HIGH PRAISE FROM DOWN UNDER

PETER CORRIS

"There is nothing random or haphazard about the way Corris tells his story; it is a piece of masterly, disciplined and highly effective narrative."

The Australian

Cliff Hardy

"We have at last, an Australian investigator to rank with Poirot and Wimsey, with Marlowe, Lew Archer, and Sam Spade."

The National Times

Make Me Rich

Another superb look at crime and punishment featuring Australia's terrific sleuth!

Fawcett Gold Medal Books
by Peter Corris:

THE DYING TRADE

THE EMPTY BEACH

MAKE ME RICH

THE MARVELOUS BOY

WHITE MEAT

MAKE ME RICH

Peter Corris

FAWCETT GOLD MEDAL • NEW YORK

A Fawcett Gold Medal Book
Published by Ballantine Books
Copyright © 1985 by Peter Corris

First published in Australia by Unwin Paperbacks 1985
Second impression 1985

ISBN 0-449-13021-5

This edition published by arrangement with George Allen and Unwin
Australia Ptg. Limited.

Manufactured in the United States of America

First Ballantine Books Edition: June 1987

For
H.M.F.

It was just another party job in Vaucluse. Mrs. Roberta Landy-Drake was paying me five hundred dollars for keeping an eye on the valuables and the cars and throwing out the drunks gently. It was no fun working at a party, and these big money bashes were all the same. They had the same rhythm of arrival, mouths opening and closing to permit talking, eating and drinking, farewell and departure. Rich drunks are all the same too, and not different enough from poor drunks to be interesting.

But the money was okay and the work was steady and getting steadier. It seemed more rich people were having parties that year; maybe they felt better about being rich while everyone else was getting poorer. But they weren't all bastards—the generous ones might give you a half scotch and soda at the end of the night and let you stick your finger in the cheese dip.

It was the second job I'd done for Mrs. Landy-Drake; I never did find out who Landy and Drake were—ex-husbands would be a fair guess, judging from the abundant evidence of unearned income. The house had more rooms than there are names for, and if you'd backed a truck up to the door and taken away the paintings you'd have been set for life. Roberta, who got on first name terms within sixty seconds, employed people like me to keep a sharp eye out for trucks. Nothing went missing from the function I'd officiated at in the spring, so here I was, back for the summer one. It was clearly going to be easier—no furs to worry about.

Roberta, hostess of the year twice running, set the fashion style: her black dress was designed to show the maximum amount of suntan on her long, slim body. It had holes in it and scallops that made it seem more off than on. I was allowed to relate to the other help for a while—the drinks' servers and food preparers—only letting me glimpse her from afar, before her sense of drama told her it was time for us to talk. She approached me as I was accepting a set of car keys from an early arrival who asked me not to let him drive home, no matter *what* he said. She gave me her carefully painted smile and took a sip from her glass.

"You were wonderful last time, Cliff. I'm glad you could help again."

She liked the illusion that everyone was her friend and that there were no employees. Why dispel that?

"Happy to be here. Enjoy your party, Roberta."

The first flotilla of guests sailed in and the mouth-opening started. I cruised around the grounds—tennis court, pool, barbecue pit—and checked the cars—Volvos, BMWs and their cousins. Inside, I renewed my acquaintance with the Drysdales and the Nolans.

The house filled up fast, and the guests spilled out under the marquee at the back where the caterers kept the food and the booze well up to them. At 9:50 I swept up a broken glass; at 10:25 I parked a car the owner was too drunk to do anything with but leave in the middle of the road; at 12:30 I earned the five hundred bucks.

The first time I laid eyes on him I could see he was drunk, but he wasn't in charge of a car and he had all his clothes on so it wasn't any of my business. That was around 11:30; an hour later he was raping one of the guests under a Drysdale in one of those unassignable rooms. She was screaming and he was grunting. He was a big guy, six two or so, and therefore had an inch or more on me and the weight to match. His grunts were deep and rhythmic. His shirt was hanging out at the back and I bundled up a fistful of it, pulled hard and swung him up and off the blond teenager on the pile of cushions. The pull brought him around to face me; he stood unsteadily and yanked the long shirt-tail free.

"Put it away," I said, "and go home."

The blonde screamed and he grunted again as if he liked screaming. I looked away to the girl and that's when he threw a punch. It wasn't the first punch he'd thrown, he knew how to do it, but it wasn't one of his best. The booze in him made him slow and indirect; I stepped inside the swing and dug my fist hard into his belly. The wind goes out of them when you do that, and if you can hit hard enough and quick enough in the same spot they go down. I did and he did. I helped the girl up and she pulled down her dress and adjusted things.

"Did he hurt you?"

She shook her head and a panicked look came into her eyes. "Don't tell . . ."

"No telling," I said. "Go that way and wash your face."

She grabbed up a detached shoe, stepped around the cave man, whose grunts were of a different quality now, shot past me and went out. I knocked the cushions back into shape, checked that no harm had come to the painting, and turned my attention to the man on the floor.

He was vaguely familiar; I'd thought so at his unsteady arrival and the feeling was stronger now, although it's hard to place someone when he's three shades redder than usual and is lying on the carpet fumbling with his dick. I was curious to know.

"Who're you? Lover of the month?"

"Get fucked!"

"I doubt it, not tonight. And you neither. You've had enough party. Time to go."

3

"I'm Colly Matthews."

He was. It wasn't a name you'd lay false claim to. Colly Matthews was a Rugby League front row forward, a regular member of a senior side when he wasn't serving out suspensions. I'm a Union man myself, and I hadn't even seen him play, but I knew from the back pages that his nickname was "Sin bin," that he was under suspension at the moment and that there was a movement afoot to ban him for life. Or at least to ban his elbow, which would have banned the rest of him as well.

"I don't care who you are, you should ask a lady's permission first. You've got time on your hands, you should go to a charm school."

"I'll kill you," he bellowed.

"They'd work on that, first lesson."

He'd got himself back in order by this time, but every instinct told him to hit until something broke. Maybe they train them that way, I don't know. He told me to get fucked again, and I found this very boring.

"Piss off, Matthews. I'll tell the hostess you came over faint."

He might have had another go; he pulled himself up off the floor as if that was in his mind, but just then another man appeared in the doorway and some party chatter flowed down the passage outside. Matthews finished adjusting his clothing. The new arrival laughed at the footballer's buttoning and zipping; he was short and slight and not young, but laughing at "Sin bin" didn't seem to worry him.

Matthews made as if to bullock past us but I eased him into the door jamb. I could hold him there a second because I was sober and had my balance.

"Are you driving?"

"What business is it of yours?"

"No drunk leaves this party driving—that's the rule."

"I lost my fuckin' licence!"

I stepped back and let him lurch through and away. I followed him down the passage; he looked back a couple of times and I made "go" motions with my hands and steered him toward the front door like a cattle dog. A few party persons stopped talking long enough to watch us, but they mostly regarded the incident as entertainment and their response was well-oiled laughter. Some of them would have laughed at a kneecapping.

The short man past his prime had followed me all the way.

"A mess," he said, as the door closed behind Matthews.

"Yeah." I wasn't feeling chatty; drunk athletes don't cheer me up, and I turned away from him to try for a handful of peanuts or something. But he stuck close.

"Are you a fan of the game?"

It was difficult to talk to him, because to do so I had to look down and when you're looking down you're not looking around, which was what I was being paid to do. Still, what's worse than being at a party and having no one to talk to? I looked down.

"No," I said. "I'm not too keen on it; when they all pack down like they do I imagine I can hear the spines snapping. What did that bloke call it? Wrestling on the run? It's all right when it flows, but it doesn't seem to flow all that often."

"Right." He stuck out his hand. "Paul Guthrie."

We shook. "Cliff Hardy. I'm here looking after things for Roberta."

"Gathered that. Drink?"

I shook my head. "No thanks. I'll have one before I go. I'd better go outside and make sure the football hero isn't stealing the hubcaps."

He nodded. "Talk to you again."

My turn to nod; he walked away—a calm, self-assured little man with something on his mind and what looked like

5

mineral water in his glass. He looked slightly out of place in the gathering, but it didn't seem to worry him.

Everything was quiet outside. I stood near a bush with a nice, strong scent and enjoyed the cool evening air as a break from the noise and the smoke. I'd left the jacket of my suit inside, but I still felt uncomfortable in tailored pants and a collar and tie. It was that sort of party though, and in my usual get-up of shirt and jeans I'd have stood out a mile as the crowd controller. The party was up at a loud roar; a few people trickled past, going in and out. They all seemed to be having a good time, and I wondered if their lives were fuller and richer than mine. Richer in worldly goods I could be sure of; they had expensive cars and credit cards to keep the tanks eternally full. My car was old and half a tank was all it was used to. On the other hand, jobs like these had pushed me into the black economy. Some of the clients wanted to pay in cash and who was I to quarrel? I'd had a conversation recently with Cy Sackville, my lawyer, in which he'd advised me to form a limited liability company in order to protect my earnings.

"I'd make a loss," I said.

"That's the idea. The shot is to get someone else to act as a director—your brother or someone . . ."

"I haven't got a brother."

"No? You'd probably be a better person today if you did—less selfish."

"Have you got a brother, Cy?"

"No."

I hadn't formed the company, and tax problems were a possibility; even so, a year's income wouldn't buy most of the cars owned by Roberta's guests. Against that, I could have the collar and tie off in an hour and spend the day on the beach.

Back inside everything was going swimmingly—some of them were actually splashing about in the pool—and the dry

6

ones were happily getting wet in their own way. Roberta wafted up to me and put the hand that wasn't carrying the champagne glass on my arm.

"Cliff, darling. So marvellous of you—getting rid of that awful footballer. Paul told me all about it."

"Why was he here, Roberta?"

She looked at me with eyes that seemed to be focussed on something that would happen the day after tomorrow, if then.

"Why are any of us here?"

She drifted away and joined a group that was admiring the view across to Point Piper through a floor-to-ceiling window. A tall, strongly built woman with a lively, broad-featured face and short-cropped reddish hair broke away from the group and strode across the room toward me.

"Hello," she said. "Been hearing all about you. So you're the minder."

She had a deep, husky voice like a blues singer, and her party clothes consisted of a black overall arrangement without sleeves, which zipped up the front and was gathered at the ankles. There were no doo-dads on it and she wore no jewellery.

"That's just what they call it on TV," I said. "I don't get paid in Nelson Eddys or anything."

She laughed. "D'you know much rhyming slang?"

"Not much, no."

"I heard a good one the other day—'arris for bum. Know it?"

"No."

"It goes—'arris is short for Aristotle, rhymes with bottle; bottles and glass equals arse. See?"

"Yes, good. What're you, a writer?"

"No." She waved the hand that held a cigarette; a wisp of the smoke went into my face; I coughed and moved back.

7

"Don't!" she said sharply. "Look, it's a Gitane; I only smoke one a day. Don't spoil it for me."

"All right." I sniffed at the cigarette. "Wish I could smoke one a day."

"Why can't you?"

"I was a tobacco fiend for twenty years. Gave it up. Scared just the one would probably set me off again."

"Mm, might. Better not try. I'm Helen Broadway; I asked Roberta to introduce us but she didn't seem to understand what I meant."

"Cliff Hardy, hello. I think the champers has got to her. She's Brahms."

"And Liszt."

I laughed. "Right."

We moved away from other people, as if by mutual agreement. I looked around a bit, staying in touch, but most of my attention was concentrated on her.

"Apart from the fact that you're sober, like me," I said, "and that you're not wearing any jewellery, like me, I'm trying to work out what's different about you—I mean, compared with all these people." Mentally, I put Paul Guthrie in the "different" basket too.

She leaned toward a table and stubbed out the Gitane. She had a dusting of dark hair on her long, brown forearms.

"You won't guess," she said. "I'm not foreign, I haven't got cancer, I'm not a lesbian. I'm from the country."

"You're not! That's original—where?"

"Up near Kempsey, ever been there?"

I had, chasing people and being chased, some years back. Shots had been fired and a truck with people in it had gone up in flames. Not my favourite memories. But I was prepared to give the place another chance. I liked Helen Broadway.

I told her I did know the Kempsey district and we exchanged a few place names. I told her I should go on my rounds and she came with me, again by unspoken agreement. It was very pleasant; I almost felt as if I was at a party. It was cool outside; she wrapped her bare arms around herself and stood close, using me as a windbreak.

"Good name," I said. "Broadway."

"Married name. I'm separated though, I think."

"How does that work? Thinking you're separated?" We went back inside and I poked my head into a room where bags and other guests' belongings were stowed.

"Mike's given me a year off. His sister's going to look after the kid. She's twelve and she needs a break from me as much as I need one from her. I can do what I like for a year."

"How long have you got left?"

"Well, it's coming up for a six-monthly review any day. I can go back or stay on down here."

"Which?"

"Don't know."

"How about money?"

"We had a good year on the farm and in the business. Mike gave me half."

"What have you been doing?"

We were back in the main party room now; the noise level was still high but the party had thinned out. I was wondering whether Helen had an escort or whether she might like to stick around until the last reveller left. And what would my approach be? The matter was set aside by Paul Guthrie who planted himself squarely in front of me.

"I'd like to talk to you, Mr. Hardy. Excuse us, Helen."

I didn't want her to excuse us, but Guthrie was one of those experienced social movers who knew how to get his way without giving offence. I gave Helen Broadway my best we-haven't-finished-yet look before Guthrie guided me into a quiet room. There was a table covered with a white cloth which had a nest of bottles on it and some baskets and plates with crispbreads and wafers of smoked salmon and turkey.

Guthrie poured an inch of Jack Daniels into a glass and added an inch of water.

"You can have your drink now," he said. "Party's nearly over, and I cleared it with Roberta. I want to talk business. You want to sit down?"

I shook my head; I was leg-weary, but when I sat down I wanted to stay down. I leaned against a wall and took a sip of the bourbon, which tasted wonderful: I made a silent, private toast to Helen Broadway.

"You handled that rugby clown pretty well," Guthrie said. He didn't have a glass or props of any kind; he just stood there in his well-tailored lightweight suit with a soft collar and a quiet tie, and exuded his own brand of charm.

"He'd handicapped himself." I held up my glass. "That elbow of his gets him into trouble in more ways than one."

He smiled and nodded. Then the smile fell away. "How would you like to earn ten thousand dollars?"

I took another sip to give myself reaction time and looked down at him; concentrating on him now and not on the woman somewhere in another room. For the first time, I saw the strain in his face. He must have been over sixty, but his slim figure hid the fact. Now, very late at night, he had a greyish tinge and the white stubble on his face etched worn deep lines. He was old, tired, and deadly serious. That's a combination to make you nervous and send you in the other direction. Worst comes to worst, you can lay a joke over it. I took another sip.

"Who would I have to kill?"

"Not for killing, Mr. Hardy. For saving someone's life."

2

Paul Guthrie was exaggerating, of course; people usually do when they want something from you. But his problem was real enough. He was, he told me, sixty-two years old, a businessman with interests in sporting and leisure activities. He owned a couple of marinas in Sydney, leased game fishing boats to the rich, and had controlling shares in a ski lodge and a dude ranch. He used that expression with obvious distaste, which lifted his stocks with me. He'd rowed for Australia in the double sculls at the 1948 London Olympics.

"Unplaced," he said.

"Still, a big kick."

"Yeah, it was. A bigger kick was coming home through the States and seeing how they were organising things there. Business, I mean. You never saw anything like it. Marinas sprouting everywhere, airfields; lot of ex-service stuff going into recreational use. That's where I got the idea for the leisure business. It was slow to take off here, but it has now. I built it up sure and steady."

"Well, the Yanks were always long on ideas. You certainly got in early."

"Right. Too early, I thought for a while. I worked like a dog at it. Blew a marriage to pieces in the process. I got married again ten years ago. She's twenty years younger than me, and had two sons from her first marriage. They were about eight and nine at the time. I didn't have any kids, and I helped to raise those two. I think of them as mine."

The value of sentiments like that depends on the speaker. I rated Guthrie pretty high: he wasn't big-noting himself about his business success, just filling me in. And he'd put it down to work rather than brilliance—always a sign that the person is a realist. Physically, he was impressive too; there was no fat on him and he looked as if he could still pull an oar. But his problem was eating at him, sapping his reserves.

"The boys are the problem, that right?"

"One of them, Ray—he's the oldest, nineteen. Just under nineteen. I haven't seen him for four months."

"That's not so long."

"It is for the way it happened. The other boy, Chris, he went up to Brisbane at the beginning of the year. He's all right—went to university there. They've got special studies in race relations—Aborigines, Islanders and all that. That's what he's keen on."

"What about Ray?"

He rubbed at his close-cropped grey hair, making it rough and spiky. "We had our difficulties. Started a few years back. We just didn't get along as well as we once did. No serious stuff; just sulks and no co-operation. A real pain in the arse to have around."

"That's normal enough."

"So they tell me. Now, Chris could be hard to handle too but he'd go off and hit the books. Ray's no scholar. He's not dumb, mind. Passed the HSC, but he wasn't interested in going on."

I finished the drink and thought about another. I was tired, and still had some clearing up to do at the party. It was a sure bet that there'd be someone asleep somewhere to be woken up and poured into a taxi. Besides, he was reluctant to tell me the trouble and that's an attitude I've come across before. Sometimes it takes three runs before they come out with it and tonight I didn't have the time. I wanted to let him down gently, though.

"I'm sorry, Mr. Guthrie. It just doesn't sound so different from a lot . . ."

"It gets different," he said sharply. "We had a bit of a row the day Ray left. He wasn't under the thumb, you understand. Lived on the boat . . . I'm sorry, I'm having trouble coming to the point."

"You had a row."

"Yes. He stormed out. No word since. His mother's out of her mind. I asked around. Couldn't find him, and then I heard about the company he's keeping. Bloke like you would know what I mean. Apparently he's hanging around with Liam Catchpole, Dottie Williams, and Tiny Spotswood . . . that lot."

Those names changed things a lot. Catchpole, Spotswood and Williams were all crims. Not big-time enough to make their full names a household word—Liam Angus Catchpole or whatever—but consistent, professional wrong-doers. All had convictions, but it was rumoured that Tiny Spotswood had done things much worse then those he'd been convicted for. Bad enough, but there were other reasons to avoid them: I wondered whether Guthrie had the whole picture.

"Bad crowd," I said. "Bad example for an impressionable lad."

"It's not the bad example I'm worried about. Those three are police informers."

"Right."

"And steerers!"

He meant *agents provocateurs,* and he was right again. Catchpole survived by steering men into gaol. Dottie did the same with women and she had a sideline as a drugs provider and procurer. I knew Catchpole had had some connection with Glebe in days gone by, but the details eluded me. I knew of no one who trusted him—not the crims he associated with nor the policemen he provided with information. He was almost, but not quite, a pariah. Tiny's muscle helped to make people civil to him some of the time.

"Do you have any idea what's going on?" I asked. "Has the boy had police trouble?"

He shook his head emphatically. "Never. I'd have to say he's moody and stubborn—but honest as the day. And he's not lazy—worked like a bastard on the boats. In my experience it's the work-shy that run into trouble first. Ray's not work-shy." Now that he had it all out in the open, he was determined to convince me. "Look, Hardy, you know your way around. I've seen you in action and Roberta speaks very highly of you. She's a good judge of character, though you mightn't think it. I want you to take this on. Find Ray, talk to him. Find out what's going on. Get between him and that slime somehow, before he goes wrong."

"He might have gone wrong already."

"I know it. I'm prepared for that. But I'm sure Ray's basically solid. There's something . . . what do the kids say? . . . bugging him. I know it doesn't take long to go off the tracks. All the more reason to step in. Will you do it?"

It didn't take much thinking about. I liked Guthrie, and the few times I'd seen Liam Catchpole up close I'd wanted to go and have a shower. Youth is worth saving. It sounded like a more worthwhile way to make money than some of the things I'd been doing lately.

"I'll try," I said. "The money you mentioned is too much—I'll take seven fifty for a retainer, and work for a hundred and twenty-five a day, plus expenses."

14

"Bonus for results," he said.

"Fair enough."

We shook hands and I felt self-conscious as some departing guests looked at us curiously. Guthrie's hand was hard and corrugated, dry to the touch. He stepped back; he seemed almost sprightly. "Just come here to try to cheer myself up," he said. "Pat couldn't face it. I didn't think I'd do anything positive about Ray."

"Don't get your hopes too high," I said. "You can't make people be good, you can't make them be grateful, you can't make them be anything. Not really."

"Why d'you say that? About being grateful?"

"Most parents want their kids to be grateful."

"You got any kids, Hardy?"

I shook my head. "I'd probably want them to be grateful if I did. And they probably wouldn't be." I grinned at him. "Too disappointing."

"I don't want him grateful. I just want him . . . safe." He handed me a card; his colour was better already—action did him good. He checked his watch. "Ring me later today. Okay? We'll get started."

It was 2 A.M. I did a last check on the people and the silverware. Nothing seemed to be missing and when I put Mr. and Mrs. Olsson, who seemed to have shot for the "drunkest couple" title, in their cab I was through for the night.

Roberta was snoring gently in an armchair. One brown breast had fallen out of her dress and she had one silver shoe in her lap. I shook her arm gently.

"Roberta. Party's over."

She opened one eye theatrically. "Wasn't it awful?" she groaned.

"It was fine—great success."

15

"I'll send you a cheque. Thanks, Cliff." She dropped the eyelid.

I collected my jacket and took off my tie. In the kitchen I annoyed the clearing-up caterers by making myself a chicken sandwich. I took it out to the car with me, chewing slowly and wishing I had some wine to go with it. But I gave up keeping wine in the car a long time ago. As I started the engine I remembered Helen Broadway. I hadn't seen her go and I didn't know where she lived. I could ask Roberta—but not just now.

3

I got home to Glebe around 2:30 A.M. I've given up tucking the car away in the backyard; the strain of the backing and filling is too much and the local vandals seem to have decided my car isn't worth their attention. The street is narrow, with a dogleg; my place is just past the dogleg. I let the wheels drift up on to the kerb and slotted her in—slapdab outside.

I glanced at a newspaper Hilde, my tenant, had left lying around while I got a few last dribbles from a wine cask. We had a commission of enquiry into the early release of prisoners scheme on the front page, and a commission of enquiry into the conduct of boxing on the back. Both dodgy was about all the reaction I could muster. I took the glass up to bed; there was light showing under Hilde's door; I knocked softly and pushed the door open. She was sitting up in bed, reading. A long strand of her blond hair was in her mouth, and she was chewing it rhythmically as she read. She lifted her blue, German eyes reluctantly from the page.

"It's 2:30," I said.

"I'm reading *Gorky Park*."

"That explains it. Goodnight."

I slept late. By the time I got up, Hilde had gone off to do her dental research. She tells me that fluoride in the water has cut dental decay by 84 per cent, so that the emphasis in her trade these days is on preserving and presenting the dentition. When I asked her what that meant she said, "Capping and straightening." I understood that.

She'd left a pot of coffee on a low flame, and I got to work on that while I ran a routine check on Paul Guthrie through the telephone book and *The Company Index*. He lived in Northbridge, between the golf course and Fig Tree Point. It sounded like a well-preserved and presented address for a client to have. Guthrie Marinas Pty. Ltd. was at Balgowlah, Double Bay, and Newport. The ski lodge and dude ranch were probably called the Alpine this and the Western that. Guthrie Enterprises was listed as a private company; Paul Guthrie, principal.

I rang him at 10:30; he came across eager and energetic; he made sixty-two sound like something to look forward to.

"Tell you what," he said. "I have to go up to Newport to look a few things over. Like to come up? Go out on a boat?"

"Is there any point?"

"Yes, Ray kept a lot of his stuff on a boat up there. I suppose you could look through it. Must be a photo of him there—you'll need that?"

"Yes, I will. Anything else?"

He paused. "Yes. His girlfriend's there. Girlfriend that was. She's a nice kid. I talked to her, of course. Said she hadn't heard from Ray, didn't know anything. But it might be worth your while to talk to her."

"Okay. I'll meet you there. I've got the address."

He sounded nonplussed. "How's that?"

"I looked you up in the book and the commercial directory. You check out just fine, Mr. Guthrie. You got my credentials, remember? And Roberta was a little past giving you a reference last night."

18

He laughed. "That's smart. I'll give you some money. What time suits you?"

"Let's say at the marina at noon. Nothing's happened to change your mind about this, has it?"

"No. Why?"

"It sometimes happens that way. You act, like by hiring me, and something else happens. Never mind. Noon."

It was hot and Friday, which meant heavy traffic on the road and a slow, sweaty drive to Newport. I was passed by cool-looking people in air-conditioned cars and I wondered, not for the first time, whether I should get a soft top. I didn't have a woman to ride in it with me—wearing a scarf and with her sunglasses pushed back on the top of her head—but maybe I could do something about that. Roberta Landy-Drake's cheque would take care of the rent and the mortgage for a month; a couple of steady weeks work for Guthrie, and maybe then I could think about a soft top. I thought about it anyway as I drove sedately north, past the hamburger bars and surf shops, and eventually past the pub in Newport where we used to come in the bad old days with our genuine thirsts and phoney addresses, and pass ourselves off as *bona fide* travelers.

The approach to the marina was through a bumpy car park beside a pub that hadn't existed back in the sabbatarian days. I parked in a small patch of shade that would get smaller as the day wore on. The marina was an arrangement of boat sheds, office, workshops, and jetties all connected on different levels by steps and walkways. I walked down toward it, jiggling my keys and thinking ambivalent thoughts about boats.

Guthrie was waiting for me on a wooden walkway that led to the moorings. He was wearing jeans, a tee-shirt, and canvas shoes. I was relieved to see that he didn't affect the cap and scarf of the pseudo sailor, but I hadn't expected he

19

would. We shook hands and I realised that the hard ridges I'd felt the night before were from boat work. He might have sounded full of beans on the phone but he looked a little tired now, not at the peak of his form, and he was hiding his eyes behind sunglasses.

"Going out to check some of the moorings," he said. "Routine work in this game."

"Don't you employ people to do that?"

"Sure, but I like to keep my hand in. Along here, and watch your step."

The planks and rails seemed to be in good condition—no splinters, no flaking paint. There must have been more than a hundred boats tied up there—big, swank things like over-blown birds and neat, smaller craft with more interesting lines. The water was a deep green around the pylons and the boats were mostly white with blocks of red, blue and brown. The bright sun flashed on brass name plates—*Pocohontas, Bundeena, Shangri-la*.

Guthrie stepped over piles of rope and mooring lines like a mountain goat on a familiar path; I followed him carefully to where a handsome motor yacht was moored between high, rope-wrapped pylons. *Satisfaction* was painted in bold, white letters across the stern and at the bow on the side I could see. A flag was flying from a high mast and a couple of seagulls hopped along a polished rail on the side. As boats go, this was a beauty. Guthrie jumped down on to the deck from the jetty untroubled by the distance or the motion of the boat. I edged down the metal ladder a few steps, waited for the rise and stepped aboard carefully.

"Not used to boats?"

"Been a while."

"This is the one Ray used to knock about in mostly. Not in bad nick, is she?"

I nodded. Everything looked well cared-for without being

fussy. Truth was, I was accustoming myself to the motion but, to show willingness, I went under the awning that covered the rear section of the deck and looked around. I noted the life jackets safely stowed. Guthrie noted me noting and grinned.

"Don't know why, but I feel a bit better about things when I'm on the boat. Hard to believe he could go bad, the old Ray. Help me to cast off, will you? Then you can go below and poke around—look at anything you like."

We unlooped the ropes; Guthrie started and warmed the engines and then took the boat smoothly out into the channel. Although I grew up by the water, at Bronte and Maroubra, I wouldn't say I had boating in the blood. The inner tubes from car tyres were the first craft I remembered, and I didn't rate the inflatable rafts and boats we'd trained in as soldiers much higher. I spent a very tricky night and a day in one of those things up a river in Malaya, and being afloat wasn't my favourite sensation. But at least I wasn't a lunch-loser.

After doing some suitable appreciation of the scenery, I ducked my head and went into the saloon section and from there down a short set of steps to the cabin. The circumscribed space held a two-tiered bunk, built-in shelves, and a cupboard. There were two portholes and between them a shaving mirror, a wineskin, a belt with a knife in a scabbard, and a heavy oilskin were hanging on hooks. The books on the shelves were mostly paperback thrillers but there were also a few navigation manuals and an anthology of sea poems. There was a plastic coat, a work shirt, a sweater, and a pair of very greasy and stained overalls in the cupboard. The bed was neatly made on the bottom bunk; the top bunk was covered with a single blanket.

Ray's personal belongings were in a tin chest under the bunk. I pulled it out and teased open the cheap padlock with a pocket-knife blade. I turned the bits and pieces over thinking how alike we all are—how we all keep the same things, the bits of paper and objects that mark the staging posts of our lives. Ray had stored away a couple of not discreditable school reports, a learner-driver permit, a swimming proficiency certificate, a half-empty box of long rifle .22 bullets and some photographs.

I stood up from my crouch with creaking muscles, and spread the snapshots out at eye level on the tight blanket on the top bunk. There were five: one showed a big-looking, blond kid at the wheel of the *Satisfaction;* another was of the same boy with a younger and slightly smaller and darker version of himself, sitting in the yacht's dinghy; there was one of a small, handsome woman in early-middle age standing with her hands on her hips and looking amused at the camera; and a fourth snap showed a teenage girl with long legs and short shorts sitting on a low stone wall. She was smiling at the camera and displaying good teeth, shining mid-length hair and an optimistic glow. If Paul Guthrie had given me intimations of hope about getting old, she was a reminder of the joys of being young. She was the sort of girl song-writers used to write songs about before they discovered Freud and drugs.

The fifth photograph was the maverick in the bunch; it was old, not so old as to be sepia-tinted, but it looked as if it had just escaped that photographic era. It was also cracked and creased as if it had once had a less loving home. The picture showed a man in army uniform caught in the act of lighting a cigarette. He was bare-headed, short-back-and-sided and his face was half-hidden in his cupped hands. A sergeant's chevrons were on his jacket sleeve; an expert might have been able to tell from the other insignia which unit he belonged to—I couldn't. The interior shown in the photograph looked like a pub; there was a window with reversed lettering on it behind the military figure. It was impossible to tell anything about the man except in the most general terms—not old, not ugly, not fat.

I took the pictures up on deck to where Guthrie was standing with his legs slightly spread and his hands lightly on the wheel. He breathed a sigh when I spread the photographs in front of him on a flat surface in front of the wheel.

"You sound relieved," I said.

"I am. I was dreading you coming up with something like drugs or . . ."

"Nothing like that. Can you give these your attention for a minute?"

He glanced at his course, decided all was well and looked down. He came barely up to my shoulder, but his easy command of the boat seemed to give him extra stature. "No problem," he said. "What have you got there?" He stabbed one picture. "That's Ray."

"Thought so. His brother and your wife?"

He nodded.

"This the girlfriend?"

Another nod.

I nudged the old picture. "What about this?"

He peered at it. "No idea." He flipped it over as I had already done, but there was no writing on the back. I made a stack of the pictures with the one of Ray on top.

"Big lad," I said.

"Six two. No way he could've been mine—we used to make a joke of it. Chris's a bit smaller."

Six foot two, I thought, nineteen years of age and a boat worker—that meant ropes, oars and muscles. I hoped my usual verbal persuasive methods would be adequate for the task. I didn't fancy trying to make him do anything he didn't want to. Guthrie checked his course; I separated out the old photograph and the one of Ray at the wheel.

"Can I hang on to these?"

"Sure. Here we go, got to check this."

He flicked the wheel, cut the motor and brought the yacht close up to a buoy that looked like a giant, floating truck wheel. A flipped switch sent the anchor rattling down through the clear, green water. Guthrie went to the stern, hauled in the dinghy, slipped down into it and skipped across to the mooring buoy with a few easy strokes. I felt useless, so I went back to the cabin and replaced the three photos. When I got back on deck I watched Guthrie circumnavigating the buoy, pulling and testing ropes, car tyre buffers, and metal stanchions. When he was satisfied, he rowed back.

After a few more similar stops, Guthrie anchored in deep water and pulled two cans of light beer out of a cooler in the saloon. He had a plastic-wrapped package of sandwiches in there, too. We ate and drank under the awning.

"Brought you out here because I wanted you to see what kind of a boy Ray is. You think I'm pretty good in a boat?"

I was chewing; I nodded.

"He's better. Faster and sharper, and he sticks at it. One time we got a mooring rope wrapped around the propeller shaft, just before we tied up. Getting on for winter it was, dark, cold. Ray stayed in the water, down under there, for as long as it took to work the rope free. Could have cut it but he wouldn't. Bit of a perfectionist, likes to do things right. You don't see that all that often."

"That's right," I said. "You don't."

"Pig-stubborn, mind. But stubborn to a purpose."

He sucked his can dry and put it down carefully on the deck. He went into the saloon and came out with a big cheque book and a gold pen.

24

"I can't bear to think of that boy ruining his life. I can't do anything directly about it myself—too old. I don't trust the police, not in this instance anyway. All I can do is write a bloody cheque and hope you're as useful as you look and as they say you are."

"Before you write it," I said, "you have to ask yourself a few questions you might not like the answers to. Why's he hanging around with Catchpole and company? What's his trouble? If you hire me, that's what you're going to find out, maybe. The picture of him I get comes from you—he's stubborn; you won't just be able to say "stop" to him. I won't, if I find him. You might not like what happens. Your wife mightn't like it either."

He looked at me as if he was sifting the whole of his life inside his head—the good and the bad bits, and wondering how much of each there was still to come. He made a weighing-up gesture with his hands.

"I accept that," he said. He opened the cheque book, scribbled, tore out the slip and handed it across.

"That's more than I asked for."

"You don't ask enough. You're not the only one who can check up on a bloke. I checked on you. They say you stick at things and that's what I want. I want your full attention. You've got my resources behind you—if you need a thousand suddenly or whatever, you've got it. Understand?"

I nodded and put the cheque away. He seemed to regard money as something to help him get what he wanted rather than as something good in itself or something that conferred a virtue on him. That's healthy; that's how I'd regard money—if I had any.

"I've got some nosey questions up front. How much money did you give the boys?"

"Just usual pocket money. I paid them for work they did

on the boats in the school holidays. Bought them both a car—nothing flash. I give Chris an allowance to top up his scholarship, nothing much. Ray worked up here before he took off. I paid him well; overtime, the works."

"How big was the row you had? What was it about—money, politics, the future—what?"

He was stowing away the remains of the lunch and carefully brushing off crumbs into his hand. "To tell you the truth, I really can't remember. It wasn't important, nothing out of the ordinary. We rowed mostly about his attitude. I'd say, 'Don't look so bloody miserable, Ray. What's your problem?' And that'd set him off."

"Would his mother remember the particular row? Was she there?"

He thought about it for longer than seemed necessary. He took off his sunglasses and when he looked at me his eyes seemed troubled.

"I think that was it," he said. "The row was sparked off by something he said to his mother. He was just down in Northbridge for the night, stayed up here mostly . . . no, I can't get it back. But something like that. You'll have to ask Pat."

"Would that upset her?"

"She's upset already. She'll take some more if she must—to get somewhere."

He'd done enough talking. He scattered the crumbs on the water and went back to work. The anchor came up and he headed back to the marina. We swayed a bit as we crossed a bigger boat's wake, but the engines had a beautiful easy sound, and the *Satisfaction* cruised smoothly.

"Good motors," I said.

"Serviced by Ray. Exclusively."

"What can you tell me about your wife's first husband?"

Nothing happened; no sudden stiffening, no sweating, no

knuckle-whitening. "Not much. Pat didn't talk much about him at all. Divorced way back. He's dead now, I think."

"Have they got his name or yours?"

"Mine."

He was concentrating now, moving between the fairly tightly packed boats toward his mooring. I looked ahead and saw a tall figure standing by the pylons; she had a rope in her hands and was tugging at it nervously. Guthrie followed my gaze.

"This'll give you another idea of what Ray's like," he said. "That's his girl, Jess. You never met a nicer kid."

She was the young woman who'd been sitting on the wall, smiling into the lens. But now she was standing stiffly, she looked older, and she wasn't smiling anymore.

4

The deft, unhurried movements she used to help Guthrie tie up the boat seemed to be second nature to her. She was tall and athletic; the short hair, shirt, and jeans gave her a practical look and made no concessions to the usual ideas of femininity, but she was as female as you'd want—which is better. She had Paul Guthrie's full approval, apparent in every movement he made. He nipped up the ladder, hugged her and made the introductions enthusiastically.

"Cliff Hardy, Jess Polansky. He's going to look for Ray, Jess."

This news didn't seem to fill her with delight. She brushed back her light-brown hair and looked at me as if I was the understudy, not the star. "I thought . . . oh hell, I saw you take the *Satisfaction* out, and I thought it might mean Ray was coming back. Or something . . ."

She burst into tears and Guthrie eased his shoulder over for her to huddle into. She had to bend to do it. As I looked at them I tried to interpret what I was seeing. Does a son want the girl his father so obviously wants for him? It struck me that I was getting out of my depth with fathers and sons, although I was old enough to have a son of Ray Guthrie's age. As I'd told Cy Sackville, I didn't even have a brother, and my own memories of my relationship with my father weren't likely to be of much help. He was twenty-plus years dead, a quiet inner sort of man who didn't seem to approve of anything much. I still occasionally had dreams in which I tried to win his approval, and failed.

Guthrie pulled back, put his hands up on the girl's shoulders and held her at arm's length. "Talk to Cliff, Jess, give him all the help you can."

Off the boat, facing the realities on dry land, Guthrie lost some of his bounce. He let go of Jess, swivelled and spoke to me with his head turned half-away. "Ray was last seen in the Noble Briton in the Cross. Friday of last week. He was drunk. That's all I know. Stay in touch." He walked away with his hands in his pockets and his head down.

Jess Polansky wiped her eyes with her hand and looked at me suspiciously.

"What does he mean—you're going to look for Ray?"

"Just that. I'm a private investigator; I've found missing people before, quite a few."

"Ray's not really missing though, is he? I mean, Mr. Guthrie says someone saw him last week. That's not missing."

"No. You're half-right. There's missing and missing. Look, can we talk now? Would you like a drink or something?"

She shrugged. "All right. I'm on my lunch break. I might as well have a drink."

She pulled on one of the mooring lines that held the *Satisfaction;* muscle swelled and sinew tensed in her slim arm. She let the rope go and moved down the jetty.

"Ray loves that boat," she said.

"Yeah. How old are you, Jess?"

"Nineteen."

"What d'you do?"

"I work part-time for Mr. Guthrie at the marina, and I teach water-skiing."

29

That explained the muscle and sinew. "You must be good— Ray any good at it?"

We climbed steps to the walkway that took us past the boatshed. I paused and looked back down at the boats gently pulling at their ropes, rising and falling in the placid water. *Too dull for a spirited youth?* I thought. Then I remembered the order on the boat, the finely tuned engines and the anthology of sea verse. Jess Polansky moved ahead of me, exuding health and strength and I decided that Ray Guthrie couldn't have been bored here. She didn't answer my question until we were walking through the car park.

"Ray's good at everything." Her look challenged me to make something of it.

We went into the beer garden and I asked her what she wanted, expecting her to go for something soft in keeping with the athletic image.

"Gin and tonic, please."

I got one of those and a glass of white wine for me, and carried the drinks over to where she was sitting. The stone wall she sat on was the one in the photograph. I handed her the glass.

"You and Ray come here much?"

"Hardly ever; why?"

"He's got a photo of you sitting on that wall."

"Oh, I remember that. I'd got third in the state slalom titles." She gulped down a good deal of her drink, inexpertly. "Ray didn't drink much, neither do I."

The tenses were becoming confused, as if she was unconsciously getting ready to put him in the past.

"Have you got any idea why he took off, Jess? Or why he'd be drunk in a Kings Cross pub?"

"I've been trying to think. He didn't just vanish overnight, you know. He was sort of around less, always pissing

30

off somewhere. This went on for a while. *Then* he was just . . . gone."

"He didn't explain? Say what was on his mind?"

She shook her head. "Not a great talker, Ray. Quiet bloke. Terrific bloke."

It was another weighty tribute to him and I let it have its moment. I drank some wine and thought of Helen Broadway and her one smoke a day. I could've done with one now to use as I'd used them for twenty years—to help the wandering mind to focus. But I'd decided some time back that a focussing mind was no good without functioning lungs.

"What was the set up between you and Ray, Jess? Any plans?"

She had dark eyes, slightly slanted, a straight nose and a firm, well-shaped mouth. When she smiled the slant of the eyes was accentuated and her face became lively and optimistic. She smiled now.

"People don't make *plans* anymore. They just live day to day or look, say, a few months ahead. Don't you know that?"

"I hadn't thought about it. Sorry for the personal question, then. This might be another—did Ray have any unusual visitors, or mention meeting anyone out of the ordinary?"

The smile went and with it the optimism. She was getting a little out of practice at optimism. She concentrated. "I think there *was* someone like that," she said slowly. "Two men went out with Ray on the boat one day."

"What for? Fishing, or what?"

"He didn't say. They were out a fair while—all afternoon. They didn't look like fisherman or scuba divers. They wore suits."

"When was this, Jess?"

I'd finished my wine; she had forgotten her drink in the effort of remembering life. She stared past me, past the stunted beer-garden trees, straight out and up the channel.

"Hard to fix on it . . . Ray was . . ." she snapped her fingers; the sound was like a gunshot—all that water-skiing. "Got it! It was a week before I competed in the state titles. I hadn't seen Ray for a few days. I did lousy. That makes it the first week of September."

"Would there be a record of the boat hire for that afternoon?"

"Should be. A whole afternoon'd be pricey. Should be a receipt and everything. You think it's important?"

I nodded. "Could be."

"Let's go and see. I have to get back anyhow." She abandoned the drink and we went quickly back to the marina. The office was freshly painted, with new glass in the big windows; all the equipment—phones, desks, filing cabinets—were those of a prosperous business. Jess nodded hello to a woman who was talking on one of the phones, smoking, making notes, and drinking coffee. I wondered what she was doing with her feet. Jess ran out a long file-drawer, riffled through the contents and pulled out a spring-backed folder marked *Satisfaction*.

"We're computerising soon," Jess said.

"Everyone is," I said. "Except me."

She carried the folder across to a desk and started going through it, muttering, "September, September."

"Here it is!" She snapped the folder open impatiently and spread the loose sheets. There was one for each day— morning, afternoon, and all-day hirings were noted along with fuel costs, equipment hire, and the name of the hirer. In the first week of September, the *Satisfaction* had had a scattering of morning and evening hirings, with one all-day job. There was no record of an afternoon session of the kind

Jess had described. She looked at the spread sheets and then she thumped them with her fist.

"That's bloody strange."

"Describe the men," I said.

"I can't. Suits. Ordinary."

"Big or small, young or old?"

"One of each: one big, one small."

"Fair or dark?"

She shook her head. "Uh huh, don't remember."

"Anything else?"

She frowned and looked again out over the water.

"Shit, I don't know. Nothing. No! I remember now, one of them had a sort of shine to his suit. Yech! And he wore white shoes. Does that help?"

The busy woman at the other desk hung up her phone noisily. We both looked at her.

"I don't mean to stickybeak, Jess, but . . ."

"Don't worry, Val. What?"

I was amazed that she could stickybeak as well as doing all those other things. I wished I could get a look at her feet.

"Couldn't help hearing," Val said. "I saw that man in the awful-looking shiny suit. He had those terrible shoes on, too."

"You saw him when?" I said.

"Just last week. Right here. He came in here, and asked for Ray."

"What did you say?" Jess asked.

Val stubbed out her cigarette and got ready to get another going. "I told him I didn't know where Ray was. I said I wished I did know. It was *lovely* having him around here. Oh, sorry, Jess . . ."

Jess was looking upset again, frowning and shuffling the *Satisfaction* sheets. I took them from her and made a neat stack of them. Compulsive. She pulled herself together.

"Did you ask his name, Val?"

"No, sorry, I didn't."

"Don't worry," I said. "I know his name."

It was my turn to gaze out over the comforting water. Of course, he wasn't the only spiv in town; but shiny suit and white shoes precisely fitted my recollection of the unwelcome appearance of Liam Catchpole.

That gave me plenty to chew on as I drove back to the city. Big and small meant Spotswood and Catchpole, and I'd never heard that either was a fisherman, although the scuttlebutt had it that Spotswood wasn't a stranger to the waters of Sydney Harbour at night. Ray Guthrie's connection with Catchpole went back to the time when he first exhibited signs of disturbance, as the psychologists would say. But it wasn't continuous; and since Val hadn't said that Catchpole was obnoxious (apart from his suit), that meant he was on good behaviour—which meant that he was seriously concerned. It was reasonable to assume that Catchpole was a part of whatever was bugging Ray Guthrie. But Catchpole was involved in everything—drugs, prostitution, intimidation, the lot. There were no clues there, except that we could rule out anything honest.

One side of my face had got sunburned while I was on the boat; it felt flushed and uncomfortable on the drive back and it reminded me that I'd missed my day on the beach. My tan would fade; would that make me less desirable for Helen Broadway? *Was* I desirable to Helen Broadway? Did I want to be? This kind of stop-start thinking was appropriate to the movement of the traffic, which was heavy and impatient. I was weary from the gear and clutch pedal work when I got back to town. *The soft-top should be an automatic,* I found myself thinking.

A weaker man, one less dedicated to his craft, might have

heeded the over-heated engine and the ache in his bones and headed for home and a drink. But not Hardy—with a client's cheque in the pocket and a puzzler in the brain he goes on and on, like Christopher Columbus. I found myself sliding into this nonsense as the city skyline came into view. Maybe it was the motor fumes, maybe I couldn't handle a can of light beer and a glass of white wine in the middle of a working day anymore. Disturbing thoughts to be pushed aside as I ploughed on to police headquarters to have a chat with my favorite law-enforcement officer, Detective Sergeant Frank Parker. We could talk about under-convicted villains and the corruption of youth. Besides, Frank might ask me over to his pub for a drink.

Frank Parker had impressed me with his flair and imagination when we'd first met a little over a year ago. By that I mean that he didn't arrest me on principle, and didn't try to prove that he was tougher than me or better at staying up late at night answering meaningless questions in unpleasant surroundings. I'd helped him and he'd helped me on that occasion; we had a drink together from time to time, and there was an understanding between us that one would help the other again if the time came. This looked like it, for me.

I parked near the police building in a section they keep set aside for impounded vehicles. I've never had any trouble in this spot—coming or going—and I've never known why. I told the cop on the desk which bars the way to the stairs and lifts who I wanted to see, and he looked at me oddly.

"You sure?" he said.

"Yeah. Why?"

He shrugged and called the detectives' room. Parker must have given him the okay because he pointed his thumb suavely at the lifts. I rode up two levels and went along the corridor where the thick clumps of multi-coloured official paper hang off the notice boards like grapes.

I knocked on the door of the room Frank recently acquired when he moved up a grade: he only had to share it with one other detective.

"Come in, Cliff."

I pushed at the door which only went halfway before it was stopped by a cardboard box on the floor. Parker was in his shirt sleeves, shovelling papers into another box. There was a bulging green garbage bag on top of the swept-clean desk. Parker lived and worked in a blizzard of paper; it was his habitat. To see him in a bare, stripped room was a shock.

"Moving again, Frank?" I said. "You a Deputy Commissioner or something, now?"

He grinned at me and dusted his hands. "You're behind the times, Cliff. You see me at the end of what looks like being my last day in the New South Wales Police Force."

5

He filled me in at the pub—not the usual copper's watering hole, but another a few blocks from the station. He made a point of this as we breasted the bar.

"See, changing the patterns already."

"Yeah, I'm sorry about the promotion crack, Frank. Didn't know anything like this was happening."

"No reason you should. They kept it all very dark."

"It?"

The beers came and we reached out at the same time. We moved over to a window seat, out of earshot of the other drinkers.

"It's simple enough," Parker said. "I'm guilty of taking bribes. That's what the internal investigation found, and the tribunal believed. I'm suspended—I'll appeal, but it'll be confirmed. I creamed off more than fifty grand over the past few years."

"Bullshit!"

He raised his glass. "Thank you for the vote of confidence, Cliff Hardy." He took a long pull on the middy.

"What sort of bribes?"

"All sorts. For impeding the course of justice, for passing information, for intimidating witnesses."

I said "Bullshit" again, which wasn't much help to anyone.

"You don't have to tell me, mate. I've been lying awake over it for six weeks."

"What're you supposed to have done with the money?"

"There was a bookie who I placed a lot of bets with, apparently. Since gone on a long holiday—no one knows where. I bought a car and wrecked it—dealer no longer in business, it seems."

I finished my beer and tried for a lighter tone. "It just doesn't sound like you, Frank. 'Course, you never know."

"That's right, but I'll tell you this—when all this was supposed to be happening, I was too bloody tired to have a split personality."

"Set up?"

"Right." He went over for another round. Frank is a fraction taller than me; he used to be a little heavier but he wasn't anymore. The waistband of his pants was crinkled where his belt had drawn it in a notch or two. He came back with the drinks and set them down.

"I'd give the world for a smoke." His face under the blue beard-shadow had a hollow, eaten-out look.

"Fight it," I said. "Build your character. You must have some idea of why you got screwed."

"Yeah, well, to tell the truth, the problem is an over-supply of ideas. In this game what d'you make but enemies? Don't get hurt, Cliff."

"I'll try not to. Treading on toes internally, as it were?"

He grinned. "Jesus, you butcher the language. Yeah, every day. Impossible not to. Ah, I don't know. It happens. I'm not the first."

"What're you going to do? Take up drinking professionally?"

He looked at the glass in his hand. "No," he said quietly. "I've hardly had a drink since it started. No one to drink with, much. Nola's gone."

He meant his wife of ten years. I'd only met her once—had no clear image. "That's tough, Frank. I'm sorry. Was that connected with . . . ?"

"The screwing of Frank Parker? Not really. Shit, I was never there and dead tired when I was. There was no money to speak of, and no fun. She found someone who could give her a bit of both. Who could blame her? We both changed, and in different directions—I got harder, she got softer. Thank Christ we didn't have any kids."

"You still haven't told me what you're going to do about it."

"I haven't decided. Give me a chance. Let's leave me for a bit." He took a drink and gave me one of his professional appraisals. "You need a haircut. You haven't changed much since I last saw you. Why should you? You probably looked forty when you were twenty. You're that sort."

I made a fist. "I've changed inside, Frank."

"How are things—inside?"

I hadn't thought hard about it. *How were they?* I had all my hair and most of my health. I was independent. I was reading Bartlett and Steele's biography of Howard Hughes: I was better off than Hughes, but then, everyone in the bar was better off than Howard Hughes. I was all right.

"I'm okay," I said. "Working for a guy named Paul Guthrie, know him?"

Parker shook his head. "Must be a good clean job if you can tell me who you're working for."

"I wouldn't call it clean, not altogether."

"There's no such thing as really clean in your game, or in mine." He drank and snorted. "Whatever that is now. Nola said it was a dirty game anyhow."

"What's her new bloke do?"

"Search me. Why did you come to see me? You're working for fairly clean Mr. Guthrie and . . . ?"

"His son's run off the rails. Stepson really. He's put himself out of touch with the family, dropped a girl you'd run to Melbourne for, and he's keeping bad company."

"How bad?"

"Liam Catchpole, Dottie Williams, Tiny Spotswood."

"That's not good. That's trouble."

"Yeah. Catchpole seems to have turned up about the time the kid went haywire. Last week he was looking for him again. The father's been told his kid was on the piss with the three of them. You can guess what comes next, Frank?"

Parker scratched at his heavy beard; the noise was like amplified radio static. "I'd have to ask around a bit. That wouldn't be too hard, there's still people who owe me favours."

"I'd be grateful," I said.

He wasn't listening to me; he was off in the private world the persecuted build for themselves in the long, quiet nights and the slow, slow days.

"Favours . . . favours. I can put pressure on people— bucket them if I want to. They're afraid of me. Sometimes I think the whole bloody system runs on terror."

"Easy, Frank. I don't want any terror. Just a line on Catchpole—who he's fizzgigging for at the moment. What might be going on."

"Why don't you front him?"

"It might come to that. I'm just trying to be subtle first."

"Haven't lost your nerve have you, Cliff?"

"Come on, you know Liam and his sort better than I do. Thumping them does no bloody good. You make it worth their while if you can, or you find someone else who'll tell you what they won't. Thumping's no good unless you're prepared to go all the way. Liam would've got thumped in the cradle."

"You sound like a social worker."

"Just ask—will you?"

"Okay."

"Thanks. Another beer?"

"No, don't think so." He stretched his arms out in front of him and shook the imaginary bars of a cage. The old knife-scar showed dirty white on his black-haired forearm. "I reckon I'm glad you dropped by, Cliff."

"How's that? Stimulating company, I know."

"I'm not going to lie down under this. I'm forty-three, I've been in the force for twenty years. I like the work. I've got a bloody investment in it. And they owe me."

I nodded and let him talk.

"I'm going to make a stink. That's where you can help me. Tit for tat."

"Charmed. How?"

"I'd like to have a session with your journo mate, Harry Tickener. I could tell him a thing or two."

"Jesus, Frank, don't just jump into that. Think hard about it."

"Would Tickener be interested?"

"He'd give an arm and a leg."

We got up and left the pub. Parker pushed the door out and I followed him on to the street. It was early evening, still very warm, and the traffic was light. People had got to where they wanted to be. Parker stepped off the kerb to anticipate a break in the thin stream of cars. As he did, a shout of "Hey, Frank!" came from across the street. Parker's head lifted to look for the shouter, but he kept moving forward. I was a step-and-a-half behind. A green Mazda with hooded headlights left the kerb ten metres away and roared toward Parker like a blinded, pouncing beast. I jumped, and clawed at Parker's shoulder, digging my fingers in, twisting, and pulling him back. We both stumbled and he fell back on top of me. I grazed my hand breaking the fall. The Mazda screamed past.

Parker rolled off me on to his back; he lifted his head off the road. "I forgot to tell you," he said. "There's someone trying to kill me."

* * *

I went to the Noble Briton that night and on the next night, which was Saturday; both visits had their interest for a student of human nature, but neither Ray Guthrie nor Liam Catchpole showed. I made some discreet enquiries around the Cross but came up with nothing. One of the girls said she thought Dottie Williams had gone interstate for a while but was back now. Big help.

Roberta Landy-Drake had a hangover when I phoned her on the Sunday morning.

"Cliff, you're not dunning me for your fee are you? That's not classy. Especially not with the head I have."

"I wouldn't do anything that wasn't classy, Roberta. No, I wanted to know how to get in touch with Helen Broadway."

"Aha. I wonder if I should tell you. Why should you and she feel good when I feel so bad. Tell me that?"

"Come on."

She gave me the phone number and the address in Elizabeth Bay. I rang the number, but there was no answer. Well, she said she was doing what she liked and you never know where that will lead you. I wrote the address down, killed some of the day at the Dawn Fraser pool in Balmain, which they've cleaned up except for the water, and went home to make my preparations for the evening's visit to the Noble Briton. Hilde was away for the weekend so I didn't have to explain why I was having steak and Vitamin B pills for dinner on a Sunday night instead of a bacon sandwich. The reason was to erect a defence against the beer I'd have to consume to maintain my standing at the pub.

It was a mild night; I put on jeans and tee-shirt, and a denim shirt with a longish tail over that. Hanging outside my pants the shirt-tail concealed the gun I wore in a holster inside the waistband at the back. I'd splurged recently on some light Italian shoes, which were the only leather shoes I'd ever had which let me forget about my feet. In the breast pocket of the shirt I put a miniature camera which is small enough to hide in your hand and still let you pick your teeth.

I drove up William Street at about 10 P.M. The council has put up a network of barriers in Darlinghurst which block the streets off and turn them into one-way mazes. The intention and effect is to eliminate cars cruising in the area for street pick-ups. As a result, the rougher trade has moved out to William Street. The girls and girl-boys were almost jostling each other in front of the car showrooms, car accessory joints, and other businesses: three steps across the pavement takes them to the open car window where the negotiation goes on. Then it's either in and off or back across the footpath to wait for the next one. The whole transaction takes place on the front seat of the car.

A few blocks back, in the closed-off streets, the women work out of houses with doors that open directly on to the street. They don't exactly stand in the doorway with one leg up, but they aren't out in the kitchen either. There's a soft light in the front room, but that's about all the softness going.

I parked around the corner in Greenknowe Avenue and walked back to the pub in Darlinghurst Road. The Cross seemed to be operating at about 80 per cent voltage on the Sunday night. Nearly everything was open, nearly everyone who should be was there—the speilers outside the strip joints, the street girls, the cruisers, and the cops—but some of them looked tired as if the seven-day-week which is the norm for the vice business was taking a toll.

The Noble Briton is a survivor, fighting back against the homogenised, imported culture of the eighties. It has the authentic old Australian discomfort—steep, slippery steps to the toilet, cramped bar, and blind spots where the barman can't see you to serve you. The habitués manoeuvre interlopers into those blind spots. The dimness comes from the miserly low wattage of the electric bulbs rather than from any effort at cosiness.

Trade was good: there was a strong platoon of stool-sitters and bar-leaners; there was a gang of old-timers around one table and an intense young couple drinking gin at another. The pool tables were busy. I squeezed in at the bar, ordered a beer and tried to close my nose against the smoke. There was a low hum from the lubricated voices and occasional appreciative female shriek.

As I drank I tried to keep obvious observation to a minimum. Shadowy figures came and went through the door down to the toilet in processions that suggested something other than the call of nature. Men bent their heads together just out of the pools of light cast by the big tables where the cues and balls clicked. It wasn't the sort of place in which to pay too much attention to what other people were doing.

A blond woman in a pink, tight skirt that didn't come down very far over her fat thighs, squeezed in beside me at the bar.

"Wanna go along?" She shot a furtive look at the barman who had his back to us and his hands full.

"Fair go, love. I just got here."

Nothing showed in her face—not disappointment, annoyance, nothing. She nodded and moved to try further along. She watched the barman like a cat watches a bird, only moving when she judged the time to be right. She also had to watch out for other whores and pimps and predators. On the third try she scored; a tall, thin man with a prominent Adam's apple drained his schooner and followed her wide, weaving bottom out of the bar.

If you think drinking in a place where you don't want to

be isn't work, try it. I paced myself, ate chips, watched the pool games, and had a brief conversation with a man about horse racing. He told me it was all fixed; I bought him a beer and agreed. He bought me a beer and said it was all fixed.

A visit to the toilet depressed still further: the authenticity there was overwhelming—authentic old drains, authentic cracked bowls, authentic mould. The tiled floor was a Sargasso Sea of soggy cigarette-ends and discarded paper towels. A blood-encrusted sock was lying in a corner near the urinal and a trail of smeared, bloody footprints led to one of the cubicles.

The mirrors in places like that were not for the vain. I washed my hands in the thin trickle of rusty water, and looked up at a man with crinkly dark hair, a broken nose and deep grooves in his cheeks. He bared his teeth at me and said, "Cliff, you're starting to look as if you belong in a place just like this." I wanted to think of something smart to say to put him in his place but I couldn't. It was a relief to leave him there and go back up to the better company in the bar.

I worked my way back to the bar and decided to stay for the length of one more drink. The beer came and I raised it unenthusiastically—the steak and pills had probably done their work, I didn't feel drunk. I didn't drink—five metres away Liam Catchpole, with his French cuffs turned back and his hair slicked down—was gently opening his hands to let four glasses down on to the top of a freshly wiped table.

6

I'd only met Catchpole once, and then only briefly. Since then he'd had his picture in the papers. I hadn't. I knew him but there was no reason to think that he'd know me. Anonymity is an asset in my game, and I was careful to preserve it.

I took a quiet sip of the beer and surveyed Catchpole's companions. Ray Guthrie wasn't hard to spot although he'd put on weight since he stood, proud and free at the wheel of the *Satisfaction*, for the camera. He'd also grown a face-brutalising, droopy moustache. He looked prosperous in a blue silk shirt and his hair was expensively cut and styled. He was drinking beer, probably the source of the extra weight, and he'd lost his outdoors look.

The woman sitting next to him was Dottie Williams. I'd once seen a blurred newspaper photograph of her and it was enough to confirm the judgement. She had a mass of light red, curly hair, a soft round face and a double chin. She was wearing earrings that dangled near her shoulders and a frilly white blouse. The effect was supposed to be of soft femininity, but when she glanced across the bar I got a look at her blue eyes—they were as hard as hacksaw blades.

Williams kept her attention on Ray, leaning toward him, touching his arm. Like him she was drinking beer. Catchpole and the other man were drinking spirits. His back was turned to me; it was a very big back, wide at the shoulder and wide all the way down to a thick, spreading waistline.

The dark hair had departed from the top of his head, leaving him with a fringe around a bald dome. The exposed skin was very dark, so was the flesh of his thick neck.

I began to move around the bar to get another angle on the group. Catchpole was doing the talking now: four heads leaned forward toward the centre of the table like footballers in a huddle. Catchpole shut up and drank—they all pulled back and relaxed. That's when I took the first picture by cupping my chin in my hands and shooting through the opened fingers. I shifted the grip and took a few more so as not to end up with only arty finger close-ups.

The huddle again, and I moved to get a better view of the big, dark man. In profile he looked even more bulky; the depleted hair was carefully cut and his dark, fleshy face was shaved close. Everything about him—his business shirt with the gold cufflinks, the quiet tie with gold bar, the trousers so well cut that his pockets sat flat and his gut didn't stretch the pleating, said *cop*.

The crowd in the bar had thinned out a bit; I wanted more pictures, but if he was a cop it wouldn't be a good idea to be caught candid-cameraing him in the Noble Briton. He turned toward me and I took a chance; knuckling my eyes, I got one of him almost full-face. He had a meaty nose and a puffy, down-turned mouth. This guy had changed a lot, and all for the worse, since his mum had had him on her knee.

I tucked the camera away and backed off, leaving the next move to them. Their move was to have another round of drinks and do some more talking. Williams and Ray Guthrie stayed in eye contact; Catchpole and the man who I had privately dubbed "the cop," talked intently, occasionally consulting the others. There was nodding and head shaking. I didn't think they were discussing existentialism, and I would have loved to know what they *were* talking about, but there was no chance of that. Catchpole and "the cop" were evidently old hands at the discreet conversation. Liam would have picked up the elements in the slammer.

When they got ready to go it seemed to be at "the cop's" say-so. I had my back turned as they went past me and I let them get well clear before I followed. Catchpole had on the white shoes which were his trade mark, and they twinkled in the multi-coloured lights from the shop windows as he trotted along. He was shorter than Dottie Williams, who was a head shorter herself than the other two men, even in her high heels. She was wide in the beam and wore a tight skirt with a split in the back; she and Guthrie fell back behind Catchpole and "the cop." She tottered on her four inch heels, Ray steadied her and once she let her hand drift out and touch him on the buttocks.

The streets weren't crowded and the road traffic was light; I was quiet enough in my Italian shoes with the rubber heels, but I kept well back and thought about crossing the road to tail less obviously. They were about fifty metres ahead when, abruptly, they turned a corner. I heard a car door slam and I increased my pace. I rounded the corner, hugging the building line: the two men waiting for me had arranged themselves across the footpath to block me. They were both big, one in shirtsleeves, the other wearing a jacket and tie.

"Stop right there, you!" The jacketless one held up his hand like a traffic cop.

I didn't stop. I side-stepped and tried to get around them on the road. A car turned the corner then and crowded me back toward them. The man in the shirtsleeves told me to stop again; he wore a pistol in a hip holster and he had the cop's voice as well as gestures. I had a pistol too, but if you're smart you don't duel with the police in the Cross after dark.

In fact, if you can, you run; which was what I did. They were both bulky and slow and the adrenaline rushing

48

through me countered the alcohol, or perhaps blended with it and made me nimble. I feinted to one side, ducked under the swinging arm of the man in the jacket and got past. *If they shoot, I'll stop,* I told myself as I ran down the steep road. They didn't shoot and they didn't shout a warning, which told me that their business wasn't legitimate. The camera bounced in my pocket, the beer swilled in my belly and the gun stuck into my backbone. But I had my light shoes on and I felt I could run, because they were running after me.

The two of them clattered behind me and I heard one wasting his breath with a stream of obscenities as he ran. It was downhill and around the corner and into Elizabeth Bay Road. I had a discouraging flash of memory of the one time I'd run in the City to Surf race; I'd fallen twice and pulled up lame, but I kept going then, and now. Now seemed about a thousand times more important. I had good wind, the product of my year off cigarettes, and was fairly fit from regular tennis with Hilde; I felt I was gaining on them. But an uphill stretch would even us out—I never was any good on the hills.

The streets were empty of people and cars. A man sitting on a bus stop bench said something as I ran past but I didn't catch it. It certainly wasn't "I'll take care of this." I wanted there to be more people to cut down on the risk of shooting, but everyone was inside worshipping the VCR. All I could do was try not to run in a straight line.

I risked a look back and saw that I had gained some more, almost enough to think about hiding. My heart was pumping and the breath was loose in my chest. I didn't have much more left in me. I avoided the street that led down to the dead-end of the water, turned a corner and the street name jumped out at me—Billyard Avenue. The street where you live. I had the number in my head and I sprinted for it, trying to get there before they made the turn. The building was a huge, white pile in which one architectural style seemed to give way to another as it went up. The entrance was a deep portico, a lousy permanent hiding place, but adequate for temporary concealment. I gambled. I ducked in, checked her name on the tenant list and nearly fractured my finger ringing the bell.

Be home, lady, please, I thought.

"Yes." Her voice on the intercom was deep, with no sound of sleep in it.

"Helen," I croaked. "It's Cliff Hardy—from the other night at Roberta's. Let me in, please, urgent!"

"But . . ."

"Please, let me in!"

The buzzer sounded loud enough to wake the street; I said "sshh" to it, idiotically, and went through the door and flattened myself against the wall inside.

I waited for the running footsteps; they came and they turned into walking footsteps and lost any rhythm. My breath was a harsh pant, and my eyes suddenly started to stream from the effort I'd put in. The footsteps retreated. I eased off then, and put my hands on my hips to allow my chest to expand, the way runners do after a race. Running away from danger is hard work. Then I looked around.

There was a deep carpet under my feet and a chandelier overhead, two chandeliers. The moisture in my eyes was blurring everything, and my gasping breath was making the images jump. I was in a wide passage which led to a wide set of stairs. The stairs and balustrades were of old wood the colour of blood, highly buffed. The place smelt of wood polish, fresh paint, and money.

Helen Broadway appeared at the top of the last flight of stairs. She was wearing a cream-coloured garment somewhere between a nightdress and a dressing-gown. It came all the way down to her brown, bare feet.

"Don't be frightened," I said.

"You're talking to yourself. I'm not frightened."

She came down the stairs in two hops, lifting her legs and making the robe move with her—it was silk and it rustled. She looked good enough to make a full-length movie of, just her coming down the stairs.

"I love this city," she said. "Always something happening. What's happening now?"

"I'm running away from some men with guns." I wheezed a bit as I spoke and my legs suddenly felt rubbery. "No, I've got that wrong. I *was* running, now I'm hiding."

She reached the bottom stair and came across to where I'd gone back against the wall for support. The silk rustled some more and her feet made no sound on the carpet.

"How far did you run?"

"I don't know. A mile?"

"You can't be all that fit. You don't jog? I thought a man in your line of work would jog?"

"No, I don't jog. Men in my line of work mostly sit around and drink. That's what I was doing before I started running."

"We'd better call the police."

That sent me back against the wall as I tried to laugh and wheeze at the same time. I bent over and convulsed for a bit, then straightened up. She looked at me coolly.

"Finished? Are you going to tell me about it?"

"Sorry. I phoned you yesterday, or was it today? I forget. You were out."

"I do go out, yes."

"I'm bloody glad you weren't out just now."

"What would've happened—if they'd caught you?"

"I hate to think." Saying "think" made me do it, but slowly and out loud. "They'd be gone by now. They might get to my car, though."

She moved back toward the stairs. "You'd better come up and do some more thinking in comfort."

How many invitations was I likely to get to go upstairs with beautiful graziers' wives wearing silk robes? This was my first. I followed her up with legs so shaky I had to think about each step as a separate enterprise. When we reached the top she turned and saw me patting the pocket of my shirt.

"Why are you doing that?"

"Camera. I was taking pictures earlier."

That didn't sit too well; she made a face. "It's not some nasty divorce thing, is it? I thought that went out with Askin."

I laughed. "No; it's nasty, but nasty in a different way."

She grunted and led me down a hallway to where a heavy, panelled door was standing open. She waved me in and shut the door behind us.

"Go right through; the grog is in the kitchen on the left."

The kitchen was basically old style, but with enough new style in it to make it functional and comfortable. There were cork tiles on the floor and the room was big enough to hold a pine table, a two-door refrigerator and a dish washer easily. My legs weren't good; I pulled out a bentwood chair from the table and sat down.

"D'you mind if I sit down?"

"No, you're not going to faint, are you? I've never fainted myself and I don't know whether I could cope. I can't remember whether you put the head back or down between the knees. I'd probably break your neck."

I grinned at her. "I'm not going to faint. Don't think so, anyway." I put my hands on the table; they weren't shaking, I could take pride in that. "Did you say drink, Helen?"

"Yes." She went to the cupboard above the bench to the left of the sink and opened it. It was high up, and she didn't have to tip-toe. "Whisky, brandy, what?"

"Whisky would be good."

She reached up for the bottle; the silk rode up over her hips, which were wide, and showed her ankles, which were slim. The bottle of Haig was two-thirds full; she put it on the table and got a couple of glasses from the draining rack.

"Water? Ice?"

I shook my head. She poured two drinks and I put some down my throat quickly, letting it burn. She sipped.

"So," she said.

"Well, I'm glad I met you the other night; I'm glad you were home; I'm glad you let me in; I'm glad you didn't have anyone with you. What were you doing—up this late?"

"Reading. I'm glad about all that, too."

"I can't say I'm glad I got chased down your street; but, you know . . ."

"Why did you go into that fit down there when I asked if I should call the police?"

"They *were* the police. I think."

"Oh."

I finished the whisky and she gave me some more.

"Are you going to smoke your Gitane now?" I asked.

"Why?"

"I thought you might blow some smoke in my face—even let me touch it, maybe."

She laughed. "Is it really that bad?"

"Almost."

"I've had it already, the Gitane."

"Ah."

"But I'll have another just for you. It doesn't do to stick too closely to your principles. Besides, I feel nervous."

She went out of the room and came back with a soft leather bag with long drawstrings. She fished in it, pulled out the blue packet and lit up.

"Ah," I said. "That's better."

That set her off laughing and coughing. She waved the

hand with the cigarette in it helplessly, looking for somewhere to drop it. I got up and took the cigarette, then I patted her on the back and she came out of the coughing fit, laughing softly. The patting turned into embracing; I put my arms around her and we kissed. Her body was big and strong, and we kissed hard. The kiss was short—we were both recovering from loss of breath.

We sat down at the table; I handed her back the cigarette and she butted it immediately. I leaned forward and put my hand under the loose sleeve of her nightgown. Her forearm was warm; I plucked at the dark hairs on it.

"That's nice," she said. "I liked you the minute I saw you."

"Same here, me—you."

She smiled and small wrinkles fanned out from the corners of her eyes; there were faint lines beside her mouth too. I found the lines much more attractive than smoothness. I touched her face.

"Want to go to bed?" she said.

"Yes."

"You think that's a bit quick? Should we discuss herpes?"

I said "No" and kissed her again. She leaned into it; either we were getting our breath back or getting better at it. The kiss lasted longer and meant more. We stood up and hugged. I felt her hip bones bite in just below mine.

"Not too quick?"

I shook my head and kissed her neck. She twisted free and pulled me by the hand.

"I told you my first six months were nearly up," she said.

7

I wouldn't say it was anything spectacular the first time. I tend to take my cue from my partners, and my last partner had been the passive, easily pleased type; Helen was energetic, so there were some adjustments to make. She had a queen-sized bed and we used the whole of it trying to find out what each other liked. That involved a good deal of laughing.

She had black satin sheets on the bed and, after the first session, I propped up above her on one elbow and arranged the edge of the sheet exactly halfway across her breasts which were flat as she lay on her back. I smoothed the sheet down around her body and sculptured her into a sort of mermaid shape. She smiled up at me.

"Kinky," she said.

"No, just tucking you in."

"Tuck me in some more."

I did and tucking got to touching and we used our hands on each other urgently which, as it turned out, we both liked.

After, she got us drinks and brought them back to the bed. "Pretty good?" she said.

I nodded. "Very, very good. Tell me about your life."

The drinks were pretty heavily diluted with water, which is the way I'll always take my second whisky, by preference—especially at 2 A.M. She took a healthy pull on hers and looked up at the high, off-white ceiling. *Good teeth*, I thought, good everything.

"Where to start? Great question though. Ah . . . my kid's name is Verity. Sorry."

"So you should be. Poor kid."

"I bowed to pressure."

"Uh huh. How long've you been married?"

"Twelve years, nearly thirteen."

"This the first time you've been allowed out?"

"It's the first time I've been *allowed* out as you put it, yes. It's not the first time I've *been* out."

"You've had affairs with men before?" I arranged my face to make sure she knew I was joking.

"Affairs and . . . honourable stand-offs."

"I won't even ask what that means. Are you going to trifle with my affections?"

"Probably." She slid her hand under the sheet. "I'm certainly going to trifle with these."

It went on like that until close to dawn. I slept for a while, and when I woke up I was alone in the big bed. There was a small wardrobe in one corner of the room, an upholstered chair with clothes thrown over it, a low table near the bed carrying a stack of books—no other furniture. The heavy curtains over a big window were only half-drawn and light was coming in strongly through the gap. I got up, jerked the curtains apart and was hit in the eye by the view of Elizabeth Bay. The sky was an intense blue and there was a light swell which kept the boats moving at their moorings in a slow, rhythmic dance. From this distance the Darling Point shoreline looked green and unsullied. I went back to the bed, pulled up the pillows and sat and looked at the dancing boats.

Helen came in carrying a breakfast tray; she was wearing the silk thing again and it only looked better for a few creases. As I watched her it struck me that her features looked very different in the natural light. Her nose was still nicely crooked and her dark eyes deep with the fine lines ready to appear; but a tightness was gone, and the pugnacity was reduced. Sex and a little sleep seemed to do her a power of good. Her hair was spiky and sticking up irregularly; I wanted to smooth it down, groom her like a cat.

"I thought you'd be a coffee rather than tea man—toast not cereal, honey not jam."

"Right three times."

We settled the tray on the bed, kissed briefly and got into the food.

"Did you tell me anything about the job you're on last night? I have this weird memory; I forget almost everything I'm told immediately and remember it all much later."

"No, I didn't tell you."

"Are you going to?"

"What's the point?"

She laughed. "Oh, I can react all right at the time I'm being told. My understanding's not impaired."

"I'll decide according to the quality of the coffee."

I drank some and she looked at me expectantly.

"Well?"

"The coffee's good—that means I don't have to tell you. It'd be a punishment to be told about it." She punched me lightly, but a light punch from her was a fair tap.

"All right, all right, I'll tell you."

"It's just that I saw the gun, you see. Do you really need to carry a gun around with you when you work?"

I shrugged.

"I've never fired a gun in my life," she said.

"You're not missing much. I thought all country women kept guns in the kitchen. By the stove. Dumb place to keep it, come to think of it."

She'd drawn away a bit on the bed and she drank some coffee before answering. "I'm not a country woman, originally. I grew up in Sydney and only moved up there when I married Mike."

"That'd be when you were about twenty-two."

"Twenty-one; so you really *are* a detective?"

I grunted. "So-called. Mostly I go along with people when they move money about, or do things like you saw me doing the other night. I look for missing people, too. That's what I'm on now, sort of."

"You don't have to tell me about it if you don't want to."

"No, I don't mind. He's not really missing. I saw him last night in fact. He's the son of the guy who took me away from you at Roberta's. Remember?"

"I do. I wasn't pleased. I met him, Mr. . . . Guthrie?"

"Yeah. Well, he's hired me to find out what's gone wrong with his kid. There's something bloody funny about it, that's for sure. I followed the kid and the people he was drinking with last night, and that's when I ran into the two unfriendly guys I dropped off at your front door."

I put my cup down, took hers and put it down and gently eased across the bed. I licked my finger and smoothed down her hair.

"I'm not a gunman," I said. "I'm not a thug."

"I know."

"Once in a while things get very heavy in what I do—not very often, not even once a year. I haven't got a thing about guns. I got a bellyful of guns in the army."

She grabbed my face, squeezed and kissed me—she was a very physical woman. "We'll leave the army for later. I don't think I could remember any more."

She lifted her arms and I pulled the robe up and off. We remembered some of the things we'd done in the night and tried out some new ones.

Later I showered and dressed, and wandered around the flat scratching at my heavy beard. She made a few phone calls, and her movements suggested that it was time for me to be on my way. I helped her pull up the bed; we stood on opposite sides of it and looked at each other.

"You're smiling," she said. "You don't do that all that often."

"Wait until you know me better. Sometimes I smile all day. Do nothing else."

"I'd like to see that."

For her, that was a commitment. I felt I could presume just a little. "You'll see it. What're you going to do today?"

"Going out—lunch."

"What's a good time to ring you?"

"No special time. I'm busy being free. Why don't you give me your number? Let impulse rule."

I wrote the number down for her, and she let me out of the flat and the building. I could feel myself smiling again as I walked down the sunny street.

I took a good look along Greenknowe Avenue and around a few corners before I approached my car. It was after 10 A.M. and the parking ticket was fluttering on the windscreen. There was no one watching the car that I could see. I drove to St. Peter's Lane and left the car where it costs me ten bucks a week to park rather than twenty-five a night, and went up to my office. I was still smiling and even whistling—something that gives pleasure to no one but me—as I climbed the stairs.

No water view here, no high ceilings with plaster roses and soft, off-white paint. The office has cream-coloured walls which are trying to turn green of their own accord, and a ceiling so stained and dirty it looks as if it could once have been the floor. The filing cabinet has a typewriter sitting on it with a cover to keep the dust out; nothing keeps the dust off the windows or the desk top. You have to pay for a view and plaster roses and clean paint—the dust is free.

I wrote out a cheque for the parking ticket, put it in the envelope provided, and felt virtuous. I entered the fine in a notebook under "expenses" and felt businesslike. There weren't many entries under "expenses," and I couldn't decide whether to feel economical about that or non-industrious. I took the spare electric razor from the desk drawer and went down the hall to shave and clean up. A quick wash and mouth rinse, and I was ready to add something to the expense list.

I sat in my swivel chair that has given up swivelling, put my Italian shoes up on the desk and thought about Helen Broadway. I wanted to ask her what part of Sydney she'd grown up in, and what she'd been doing on 11 November 1975. I wanted to know if she played tennis and if she'd read *The Great Gatsby*. I wanted to know what she liked to eat besides toast and drink besides coffee and scotch. But right now Paul Guthrie was paying and I'd have to wait until I was on my own time.

Primo Tomasetti, the tattooist who rents me my car-parking space, has a dark room in his place of business. If walls could speak, those of his darkroom would tell Z-rated stories. I walked into the tattoo shop, held up the film cassette from the miniature camera and Primo nodded. He was working on the very large forearm of a biker who was watching the work, with his lips moving. The needle buzzed like a tormented bee.

"What's that, Primo?"

He kept his dark head with its wild, uncombable curls bent over the arm. He looked up to a sheet of grubby paper with typing on it and then back to the job. His white coat was spotless as always, he wore Italian shoes too but his were pointed.

"Rules of his club, Cliff."

The biker glowered at me and pushed back his thick, greasy hair with his free hand.

"Good idea," I said. "What's the first article?"

Primo looked up enquiringly at the customer who gave

him a sullen nod and me a look of hostility mixed with suspicion. But he was pleased with what was happening, and it made him half-civil.

Primo tested his handiwork by reading directly from the skin: "No member shall use a machine of under 1500cc."

"That lets me out," I said. "Everything set up in the darkroom?"

The camera uses a standard 15mm film, and processing these days is child's play even to the technically handicapped like me. I did the things you do with the solutions and pegs and fixative and came up with my usual result: two of the four profile shots were blurred, the others were okay. Only one of the almost full-face shots was worth looking at but it was pretty good. You wouldn't have called "the cop" photogenic, but the camera had caught the full venality of him, the forcefulness of the fleshy face and malevolence of his downturned mouth. The face stood out clearly against the indistinct background—if you knew him in life you'd know him from this picture.

I ran off a few copies, cleaned up my own mess the way my mother taught me, thanked Primo and went off to phone Frank Parker. He was at home, doing nothing, and invited me over to see him.

"Bullet-proof vests?" I said.

"Tennis gear, we'll have a game."

Frank's place was in Harbord and the suburb looked particularly well on the clear, bright day. The street was middle-income, middle-mortgage territory. Frank's house was one of the smallest; he must have been one of the few residents without children. Signs of them were everywhere around the other places—bikes, toys, and icy pole wrappers trapped at the feet of gate posts.

Frank was already in his tennis clothes; I went inside and changed into the down-market tennis gear I keep in the car—and we walked a couple of blocks to the local courts.

Parker's house had a strange, alien air to it and he seemed glad to be out on the street. He was nervous though, and he bounced the balls continually on the walk.

The three cement courts had good surfaces and clear markings. Parker spoke briefly to the manager, who lived in a house beside the courts in what looked like happy semi-retirement. The nets were in a big box; Parker dug one out and we got set up. There was no one else around to play and it occurred to me that Parker was a sitting duck if someone wanted to take him out now. I mentioned this while we were measuring the net.

He whacked the top vigorously. "Anyone thinks I'm going to sit around going crazy, they can think again. I'm not sure those go's at me have been fair dinkum anyway." We satisfied ourselves about the net height and Parker nudged his racquet cover with his foot—the shape of his pistol was clear under the vinyl.

It became obvious almost from the hit-up that Frank was about a 10 per cent better tennis player than me. His backhand was confident, mine isn't. He'd even learned how to impart some topspin to it, a thing unimaginable in the days when I learned to play. Against that, he had a tendency to hit his serve too hard which made him liable to double fault. He had quickness and range at the net, but lobbing was my forte.

It was a beautiful day, and Liam Catchpole and murderous Mazdas and police corruption seemed far distant things as we played. We both had authoritative forehands, and some of our best rallies were of that standard that lifts you out of yourself and gives you a glimpse of what real sporting excellence might be like.

Frank won the first set 6-3; I pegged him back in the second when the double faults began to creep in and I got a good percentage of my lobs over his head and in. At 6-all we decided to play a lingering death tie-breaker, which I won 9-7.

It was good to be walking back with a sweat up, despite the beginnings of a blister on my hand. Frank had stopped bouncing the balls.

"Kenny Rosewall grew up around here," he said. "Played on those courts."

"Yeah? I wonder where he is now?"

"Dallas, Miami, one of those places."

"Ever see him?"

"Bloody oath. I saw him beat Hoad for the Australian title in 1955. Straight sets."

"Remember the score, Frank?"

"Never forget it: 9-7, 6-4, 6-4. Amazing man."

"That's right. What d'you think of Cash?"

We talked tennis until we got back to his empty house. I showered and changed, and joined him in the kitchen.

"I don't eat lunch," he said. "How about you?"

"Don't care. How about some coffee?"

"Right. Can you get through to six without a drink?"

"If I have to."

He laughed. "Same here. But I'm doing it. Worst possible thing for a man in my situation would be to go on the grog. I haven't done anything about your enquiry yet. Anything new?"

The kitchen was small compared to the one in Helen's flat; it was more modern but, oddly, less practical. There seemed to be gaps in the equipment, and a shortage of spoons and crockery which reflected the departure of Nola. The bathroom had a spartan, austere air, and it looked as if the rest of the house would rapidly get that way too. Frank made coffee in a twelve-cup filter machine, and he did it neatly and efficiently, as if he enjoyed it. All Parker's work that I had seen was neat and efficient.

He poured two big mugs, set the milk and sugar down on the table and eased down into a chair.

"Pretty fair work-out," he said.

I put my photographs on the surface and swivelled them around to face him.

"That's young Guthrie," I said. "You'd know Catchpole and Dottie Williams—question is, who's the other joker?"

He sipped his coffee and studied the pictures carefully. The coffee was strong, but a touch bitter. I wouldn't have minded some lunch—you can't be too careful about getting a low blood sugar level.

"He looks familiar, but I just don't know. He's a cop, wouldn't you say? Or was."

I hadn't considered the "was" angle. "That was my impression. I didn't speak to him, mind."

"I'm not surprised. He doesn't look as if he'd go in for the small talk all that much. Where was this, by the way?"

I told him about the events of the night before, editing slightly. Parker was smart enough to do his own filling in. My account upset him: I'd seen an academic learn that one of his students was a spook and a union leader find out that his right-hand man was in the pay of the bosses. Frank's reaction to my tale of the two police types in the Cross affected him the same way.

"You didn't hear anything, I suppose?"

"Shit, no. I kept my distance."

"Wise. You should know what to look for; did you pick up anything at all from the way they acted?"

"The dark guy's the boss. There's something on between Dottie and the kid—she was feeling his bum."

"Brilliant. Can I keep one of these?" He took one of each photograph.

"Sure. Look, this might be indelicate, but I'm on good expenses for this job and . . ."

"You wound me, Hardy. You wound me deeply."

8

We left it that Frank would get in touch with me as soon as he had anything useful. I told him I'd have a word with Tickener about a former senior police officer prepared to make revelations. I couldn't tell whether or not Parker was serious about that; it would have gone against at least one of his prejudices—a belief that all journalists were frustrated somethings-else; and therefore untrustworthy. The tennis, the lunch-skipping and the abstinence suggested to me that Parker had action in mind rather than talk.

When I got back to Glebe it was after four o'clock, much closer to six than twelve and, therefore, by that logic, time for a drink. I changed my underwear and socks and tucked the denim shirt into my pants—a complete re-vamping of the wardrobe for me. The gun was in a clip under the dashboard of the Falcon. I was working on a big white wine and soda, sucking at the ice, when the phone rang. *Helen Broadway,* I thought, no, not yet.

"Hardy? This is Paul Guthrie."

"Yes, Mr. Guthrie?"

"Ray's been here. Everything's a shambles. Could you come over?"

"Where's here?"

"Northbridge; you've got the address!"

"I'm coming. Anyone hurt?"

His voice was a bitter rasp. "Physically, no."

I gulped down the rest of the drink and hurried out to the

65

car. It wasn't a good time of day to negotiate the approaches to the Harbour Bridge, the bridge itself or the exits, and the going was slow. The traffic stayed sluggish on the other side and it wasn't familiar territory to me. I had to jockey for the correct lane and I'd forgotten that the Cammeray bridge goes over parkland, and not water. But I found the turn-off and followed the golf course boundary into the heart of the suburb.

As I passed the big houses with the occasional private tennis court and the almost obligatory boat in the drive, I tried to interpret the message in Guthrie's voice. All I got was a distress signal.

The houses got bigger as I approached Guthrie's address; the driveways got wider and the gardens began to resemble private parks. As befitted a man who had made his pile, Guthrie had a house in the prime position. It was at the end of a point and had a water frontage—that's where the house would be seen to best advantage, from the water. The non-aquatic entrance was at the back where a wide, gravel drive swept in under old peppercorn trees to a shaded yard as big as a three-hole gold course. I parked with the other cars—a Fairmont and a VW Passat—and went up the railway sleeper steps to a bricked patio that held a lot of outdoor furniture and a big barbecue. The swimming pool was away in a corner near the tennis court.

Guthrie had the door open for me before I reached it. We shook hands and went down a short passage to a sunroom with cane chairs and a rug over polished boards. Guthrie was wearing old slacks, sneakers, and a tennis shirt. His short hair, usually brushed flat, was sticking up; there were deep pouches under his eyes.

"D'you want a drink or something? Thanks for coming."

"That's okay. No, no drink. Just tell me what happened."

"Ray came storming in here a few hours back. Right out

of the blue. He'd been up to Newport, and he was raving about his stuff on the *Satisfaction* being disturbed. Furious about the photos you took."

"What did you say?"

"He didn't give me a chance to think. I lied—said I didn't know anything about it. I said I'd looked through his things, but that was all. He got me so angry I didn't mind lying. That boy's in trouble."

"How did he behave, was he violent or anything?"

"Seemed on the brink of it the whole time—crashing and banging. He called me for everything then he sounded off at his mother and that got me going. She was shocked, just by the look of him."

"How's that?"

He ran his hands through his hair, which produced the sticking-up effect. "He'd been drinking. Wasn't drunk, but affected by it. I never knew Ray to have more than a couple of drinks. He seems to have got older all of a sudden. It's funny thing, as your kids get older you just adapt to it on a day-to-day basis. Bit of a jolt when you get it in a lump. And that bloody moustache . . ."

"What did he say to his mother?"

"I didn't hear much of it. I tried to calm him down, but she asked me to leave them alone for a bit while she tried to talk some sense into him. I don't know what he said but pretty soon he's shouting and stalking out of the house like a lunatic and she's in her room crying. God, I wish Chris was here; he'd show some sanity!"

Guthrie looked like a man out of his depth, or like someone called on to do something foreign to his nature. It sounded as if he'd lost his temper pretty quickly: I tried to imagine a confrontation between the neat, compact little man and the moustachioed individual I'd seen the night before. It seemed like a bad mix of characters and styles.

"Did he see Jess when he was up at Newport?" I asked.

"Don't know. If he did, he didn't say. Is it too soon to ask you what you've been doing?"

I gave him a quick report and showed him the photos. He put on a pair of gold-rimmed spectacles to allow him to study the picture of the dark man more closely. He shook his head and handed it back.

"Don't know him. Never seen him. Was Ray drunk?"

"No, they only had a couple of drinks."

He looked at the group picture again. "Something between him and the woman?"

"Yes."

"God help him. I wish you could have followed them."

"I tried."

"It's the police angle that worries me as much as anything."

I nodded. "Someone raised the possibility of ex-cops."

"God, is there anything worse?"

"Not much." I felt disloyal to Parker and others by saying it, but there was a lot of truth in it. This thing was going to get worse before it got better; and I couldn't see any point in softening it up for him. "Did you tell your wife about hiring me?"

"Yes. She seemed to think it was a good idea."

"You didn't tell Ray?"

"No, but . . . I think that's one of the things he was ranting about. Something about being followed. That must be about you and the other night. He might've accused Pat of putting someone on to him. It's all pretty confused in my head now."

"I'll have to see her."

He unhooked the spectacles and looked at them as if he hated the evidence of his ageing. Then he shoved them into the shallow pocket of his shirt, where they dangled precariously.

"I'll talk to her. Hang on."

We'd had this exchange standing up in the middle of the room. One wall was taken up with framed photographs and another by a bookcase which held a clutter of books and magazines—mostly about boats. I wandered over to look at the photographs. The oldest one showed Guthrie with a boyish physique at the oar in a scull along with his partner who looked almost identical. They had the toothy grins of young title-winners. There was a picture of Guthrie in the Olympic team wearing the dowdy uniform of those days. Then the subjects became familial and property-oriented: Guthrie, possessive and smiling, standing beside a small and pretty dark woman; two adolescent boys crewing a yacht with their stepfather; Ray Guthrie sitting at the wheel of a Mini moke.

I browsed in the bookshelf, but I'd rather look at water and swim in it than float on it or read about it, and I wasn't very interested until I came to *Technique of Double Sculling* by Paul Guthrie. It was published in 1975, not much more than a pamphlet, and it was dedicated to Ray and Chris. Paul Guthrie had taken on the role of father early and seriously.

Guthrie came back and escorted me down a passageway to a room near the front of the house. The passage turned twice; it was quite a long walk.

"She's in here," he said. "D'you want me to stay or what?"

"How do you feel about it?"

"Might be better if you have a talk on your own. He's her son." There was a lot of hurt in the last phrase and it struck me how much store Guthrie put by this family he had constructed. The threat to it was more than just a threat to

69

something comfortable and familiar, it was a threat to his future. No way to be helpful there. I nodded.

"I'll be around if you need me," he said.

I knocked on the door and pushed it open. The bedroom was full of late afternoon light through a big bay window with a deep seat built into it. There was a double bed in one corner of the room, a cedar chest, and big wardrobe with mirrors. It was neat but not too neat; there were clothes on the bed and shoes on the floor.

If Pat Guthrie had been pretty ten years ago, she was something more than that now. She had an elegant narrow head with fine, delicate features. The grey blended with fair streaks in her mid-brown hair to look interesting. She had a wide mouth that looked capable of expressing all the emotions. There wasn't much emotion showing now, though; she was sitting in a chair by the bay window, but her gaze was on the floor, not the spectacular view.

"Mrs. Guthrie," I said softly. "I'm Cliff Hardy, your husband . . ."

"Come in, Mr. Hardy. I'm sorry we have to do this in here. I just can't face the rest of the house for a while."

"That's all right." I walked into the room and she shifted the chair so I could sit in the window recess. She was wearing a white dress with a square neck that showed the intricate bones of her neck and shoulders—birdlike, but not scrawny. She was deeply tanned, and had dark eyes and eyebrows as some Celts do. I'd have bet on a Scots or Irish maiden name. There were tear marks in her light make-up and a damp spot on her dress. She was handsome; she had a fine house, a good husband and two sons. She was also deeply miserable.

"I know a bit about the background to the troubles with Ray," I said. "Can you tell me what was disturbing him so much today?"

"Didn't Paul tell you?"

"He told me about a dispute over Ray's possessions on the boat. But there's more to it than that. You tell me."

"How do you know there's more?"

"From looking at you. From the way you were looking at the floor. From the way you're looking at me now."

Her mouth moved into what could have been a smile if there'd been any warmth in it. "That's absurd. You must be a charlatan to say things like that."

"Uh huh. I'd bet what's on your mind goes back way beyond today, way beyond three months ago when Ray took off. It goes a long way back."

She'd lifted her head politely when the conversation began; although she was deeply troubled there was no weakness in the face—her firm jaw and high cheekbones were striking and strong. But she was sceptical—*Scots*, I thought, I'd have bet on Scots.

"How could you possibly know that?"

"It isn't so hard. I've seen a lot of people in distress. But really, it's just transference: if I'd been sitting and looking the way you were I know I wouldn't have been thinking about today or yesterday."

"You're right, of course. But I don't think I can talk about it to you."

"I think you have to, Mrs. Guthrie. I don't have any degrees or certificates, but I know about this kind of trouble. I like your husband. I want to help." I was carrying my photograph collection with me in an envelope—they were starting to get a little battered. I took out the one of the group in the Noble Briton and the one of the dark stranger with the bald head and the cop's walk and passed them across to her.

"Here's your son, just the other night, with two of the most unpleasant people in Sydney." I pointed to Catchpole and Williams. "And with someone else who doesn't look all that nice." I moved my finger across the surface of the photo. "Do you know him, Mrs. Guthrie?"

She glanced, looked away quickly. "I've seen the woman."

"When?"

"Today. She was in the car with Ray. I don't know the man."

I took out the old, creased photo of the Digger lighting his fag and held it for her to see. I didn't let go of it.

"You know him, don't you?"

"Yes," she said softly. "I know him. He's the boys' father."

9

"You'd better tell me about it."

She got up from her chair, crossed the room and closed the door firmly. Barefoot, she would have stood about five foot four, putting her on approximately the same eye level as her husband. She moved stiffly and bent slowly to pick up the other two pictures which she'd dropped when I'd shown her the old photograph. She handed them back to me and sat down.

"It terrifies me to see Ray with people like that," she said. "His father never drew an honest breath. Of course, that's what all this's about—Ray and Chris's father. You knew that?"

I nodded and took out a notebook to encourage her to keep talking. People sometimes make an effort when they see someone is taking the trouble to record what they say.

"What's the father's name?"

"He had a number of names. I knew him as Peter Keegan."

"How old would he be now?"

"About fifty-five."

"Your husband had the impression that he was dead."

"Yes. I encouraged that impression."

"He was in the army?"

"Yes, God knows why, probably to sell things to the other side. I think he was Keegan then. Yes, he was. I saw some papers once. What a mess."

The mess came out piece by piece: she was born in Brisbane where she'd qualified as a physical education teacher specialising in gymnastics. Six months of the Queensland education system of the 1960s was enough for her. She broke her bond with the Education Department and came to Sydney. She couldn't work in the school system, so she gave private gym lessons, did physiotherapy, coached swimming. She thought of herself as a bit of a rebel, almost an outlaw for having broken the bond.

"I wasn't really a rebel; I'd had a very conventional upbringing. But breaking the bond felt like a criminal act. Money was sacred."

"What was your maiden name?"

"Ramsay, why?"

"Never mind. Go on."

"It wasn't really so serious, breaking the bond. All they did was harass your guarantor and mine was my father, who died in the year I left Brisbane. Still, I played the runaway. Peter encouraged it."

"How did you meet him?"

"At a gym; he was hurt, quite badly. He said it was a football injury but, looking back, I suppose he did it in some brawl or other."

"What did he do for a living?"

She explained that he had presented himself as a businessman. He talked about interests in flats, hotels, other things.

"I believed it all. He had plenty of money and charm. I was flattered. It sounds absurd now, but I was a virgin . . ."

She suddenly looked directly at me, as if she was seeing me for the first time. "God, how can I be babbling like this, I don't even know you."

"You don't have to know me," I said. "It's probably

better that you don't. You need to talk to someone, that's obvious. And I'm here. I'm also very pro-Guthrie as it happens. Go on."

She smiled for the first time—a good, generous smile that let something go.

"I got pregnant and I got married. People still did in those days."

She was right, they did. I remembered how narrowly I'd missed the fate myself.

"What about your family?"

"Just a mother and a sister in Brisbane. We'd lost touch. I was in love; I didn't give them a thought. Well, Peter was good during the pregnancy, and he doted on the baby. He said that having Ray was the most wonderful thing that'd ever happened to him. I believed him—for a while."

"Then?"

"Then things I'd hardly noticed before started to bother me: where he went, who he was with, where the money came from. I started to look at him more clearly. He was a real mixture—of softness and hardness, openness and secrecy. Mixture, that's what I thought then. Schizophrenic is what I think now."

"Why d'you say that?"

"He really did know a lot about economics and money. He'd studied it and he kept reading about it—theories and practice. He did have a company too, at least one. I forget the names. But there was a wild side to him as well: he fought in pubs, crashed cars . . ."

She paused and looked past me and out the window. I swung around on the chair to look too. The light was dying in the sky. I stood up to stretch and watched the water change colour right then—it went from a pale blue to a gunmetal colour, streaked with red. She tugged at the

75

curtain but didn't close it. I sat down on the bench again, doodled for an instant and looked at her, ready to go.

"He went with prostitutes. We had a fight about that. A big fight. I couldn't understand it; I still don't. He promised to give it up and he did for a while. We got back on good terms again." Her smile this time was rueful. "Chris was the result of that."

There was a soft knock, and Paul Guthrie put his head around the door.

"Is everything all right in here?"

She gave him one of the generous smiles; Guthrie seemed to soak it up. I wouldn't have minded one myself. He smiled back.

"Just give us a few minutes more, love," she said.

"Right." He nodded at me and withdrew.

"I'd better be quick. Peter didn't keep his word. He played around all over the place. I've never understood why he got married in the first place, except that he was obsessive about children." She shook her head as if to throw a thought away. "He actually wanted a *daughter!* When all this *shit* was going on—it was unbelievable! I left him and took the boys. I went to Brisbane for a while, but the only place I wanted to live was Sydney, so I came back. I never saw Peter again. That sounds bad I know, but I haven't given you all the details. None of his businesses were legal; he had a conviction for assault and one for carnal knowledge. I felt I didn't know him. He'd told me thousands of lies. I didn't want the boys to have anything to do with him. He went overseas when he said he was just interstate. I thought he might take them away. I couldn't trust him at all. I didn't ask for anything; I just took the boys and hid. Do you understand?"

"I think so."

I was thinking how, after a relationship ends, you come to

feel that you never really knew the person at all. It must be a shock to get that feeling while the relationship's still a going concern. I'd been so interested in the story I'd forgotten to take notes. I scribbled down a few points, added a few question marks.

"How did you find out all about his criminal life?"

"I hired a private detective. I used Peter's money to spy on him. I got tougher as I went along, I can tell you."

"Who was the detective?"

"I'll never forget him. He was loathsome. His office was at 32 Mahoney Place in Surry Hills. These days I drive blocks out of my way to avoid that part of the world. His name was Phillips." She seemed to dislike even saying his name. "He knew his job, though. He wrote me a detailed report on Peter."

"Have you still got it?"

"Somewhere. I don't know . . ."

"You say you never saw Keegan again."

"No, I didn't see him, but he made contact with me. Very formal and correct. He sent me money for the boys. He didn't press to see them and I wouldn't have let him."

"When was the last you heard of him?"

"About five years ago."

She had the answer ready for the next question before I'd even formulated it.

"Yes, he kept sending money after I was married to Paul. Paul's businesses didn't really start to do well until five or six years ago. He's a very good businessman, but he's very cautious. He built them up slowly. The money from Peter was useful."

"Paul didn't know about it?"

"No."

I chewed on that for a minute, thinking what a savage

animal pride could be. She knew what I was thinking. I forced a smile.

"Well, we'll worry about that when we have to. What did Ray have to say about his father? That's what's on his mind, isn't it?"

She drew a deep breath and straightened her shoulders; the tanned skin was drawn tight over the frame of her bones and in the half-light the hollows below and to both sides of her neck looked like smears and daubs of dark war-paint.

"Ray was always more interested in his real father than Chris. That's funny, because Chris is the reflective, scholarly one. I remember I once said something to Chris about it; like, did he mind not knowing his real father. He said, 'Mum, that's the least of my worries.' It was true, too. Ray would ask about him sometimes; I'd try to fob him off. I don't suppose I did it very well. I just wanted to forget, blot it all out. But you can't blot things out for other people, can you?"

I shook my head.

"Chris thought of Paul as his father, Ray didn't. It comes down to that. Perhaps it was just the extra year or so that made the difference. A few more meetings, games . . . I don't know."

"You didn't talk about this with Paul?"

"No, never."

"So, what happened three months ago? What happened today?"

"Much the same thing really. Ray accusing me of concealing things about his father from him. Of preventing him from meeting him. Calling me a liar. It's true, I am. I did conceal things, I'd hate them to meet. I'm sure it would wreck everything. But I wasn't lying when I said I don't know where Peter was. I don't, and I haven't had any contact with him for years. Ray seems determined to find him. He's going to Brisbane to get help from Chris."

"I can't quite see why you didn't talk any of this over with Paul."

"I wish I had now. But I couldn't. I had a very bad time after leaving Peter. Some bad experiences. I couldn't believe that anyone so wonderful as Paul could exist, let alone want me and the boys. I didn't want there to be any problems. None."

"Are you saying what I think you're saying?"

"Yes, Mr. Hardy. There was no divorce. As far as I know, I'm still married to Peter Keegan."

I had to think up a story for Paul Guthrie, fast. A version of the truth is what I came out with—Ray's troubles were still unclear to us but he had talked about his brother.

"He told your wife he was going to Brisbane to see Chris," I told him after Pat Guthrie had made some reassuring noises and told her husband that she had a lot of confidence in Mr. Hardy, and that she was going to have a sleep.

"Why, for Christ sake?" We were in the kitchen and Guthrie was making tea. I hoped to avoid that.

"I don't know for sure, but it could be a good sign. The other boy's steady, you say."

Guthrie nodded and went on with his preparations. I don't mind the rituals, which look comforting as such rituals should; it's the taste of the stuff I can't stand. Guthrie had mentioned a drink when I arrived, but maybe he'd meant tea all along.

"Could you ring him up? Tell him Ray's on the way? Maybe he could get him to stay with him for a while, something like that."

The kitchen door opened and Pat Guthrie came in. "I thought I'd like some tea. What are you two doing?"

Guthrie touched her arm as if it was a privilege. "I'm making tea, and Hardy has just asked if we can ring Chris."

She shook her head. "No, he lives in some sort of student house where they don't have a phone."

"I could send him a telegram asking him to ring," Guthrie said. "Or get a message to him at the university."

"That'd take days." Pat Guthrie looked at me appraisingly and seemed to find in my favour. "Perhaps Mr. Hardy could go up there and see if he can help bring Ray to his senses. I'm worried about him ranting around, especially in strange places. I think Mr. Hardy and Chris would get along all right."

Did that make me the reflective type, I thought, scholarly, even? Flattering.

"Good idea," Guthrie said. He went across the kitchen and put his strong, oarsman's arm around his wife's slim waist. "Hardy?"

I said I'd go, got the address and details on Chris Guthrie's university courses from them, and left. I didn't have to drink the tea.

10

I got some money from the autobank at Railway Square and a surprised look at home from Hilde when I phone-booked a seat to Brisbane. She followed me as I ran around the house gathering things.

"Now?" she said. "It's night time."

"We never sleep."

"That could be true," she said. "You certainly didn't sleep here last night." I made a face at her and she went on. "And from the look of you, maybe you didn't sleep much anywhere. Mmmm?"

She was wearing a tracksuit and sneakers, prepared for one of her long, late night runs. I grinned at her and mimed running on the spot.

"Sleep or not, I beat a pennant standard tennis player 9-7 in the tie-breaker today."

"Is that so? I'm sure Helen Broadway would love to hear all about it, point by point. How was your serve?"

I grabbed her arm. "I'll break it, I swear, if you don't tell me everything you know."

She laughed and I let her go. "She rang a couple of times. Said she'd be out tonight but you could ring in the morning. Sexy voice."

"Great voice, yes. Thanks, Hilde. I'll see you."

"When will you be back?"

"Don't know."

* * *

I had my picture gallery, my gun, some clothes and books, and a collection of burglary tools in an overnight bag. If they were scanning the hand luggage I'd have put the gun and tools in a locker and go naked in the world. In my wallet I had my private enquiry agent's licence which would mean about as much in Queensland as a Fantale wrapper. I had credit cards which everyone would like, and electric shaver and a toothbrush which no one could object to.

It was late and the airport was quiet; I parked, got seat-allocated and walked straight into the departure lounge—no scanner. My fellow passengers were a mixture of business folk and family folk. A couple of kids, up too late, were giving their mother hell, and the benign smiles of the two nuns opposite only made her more agitated. Me too.

We took off on time and I ordered a double scotch as soon as I could and settled down with Howard Hughes. The kids went into first class which was a relief; the nuns were back in second class, but they didn't make any noise. I was reading about Hughes's big-fish spending to corrupt the politicians in the little pool of Nevada and trying to tell myself it couldn't happen here, when we landed in Brisbane.

I like Brisbane: I like the warm air and the houses up on stilts and the suburban gardens that are like small jungles. I hired a yellow Ford Laser at the airport, which was the least gaudy car they had. It had nothing on the clock but its springs were shot: it had a Brisbane street directory though, and at that time of night I was glad to be hiring that as well as the springs. I drove to the address I had for Chris Guthrie in the suburb of Paddington.

The same things have happened to Paddington, Brisbane, as have happened to Paddington, Sydney (and Paddington, London, for all I know): it's an inner-city suburb, once intensely working class, now saved or ruined by a middle class invasion, depending on your point of view. Unlike a lot of Brisbane, it is hilly and I noticed an encouraging number of pubs while I got myself lost in the dark, leafy streets. There had been some rain and the gardens gave off a moist, lush smell that would have gone better with the growling of tigers than the barking of dogs, which was what I got as I stumbled around looking for numbers on fence posts.

It was after midnight when I found the house: it was set high up on stilts with a lot of discarded furniture and machinery quietly mouldering and rusting underneath it. The garden was overgrown and fragrant with the wet, night smell. No dog. I pushed through the undergrowth and went up a set of rickety steps to a wide verandah. I knocked, waited, and knocked again. A light came on in the house and a frightened female voice asked from close behind the door who was on the other side.

"I'm looking for Chris Guthrie," I said.

"He isn't here."

"He does live here?"

"Yes, sort of. But he's not here now."

"Do we have to talk through the door?"

"Go away. I'm sick of people coming around at all hours for him. I have to study and I have to sleep. Go away!"

"Just a minute. What other people? When?"

"There was a guy tonight who said he was his brother and all the others for the past couple of months—the ones who look like cops, and sound like you."

"Where is Chris? D'you know? It's important."

"Will you go away if I tell you what I told the last guy?"

"Yes."

"Okay. Ask at the railway freight yard at St. Lucia. I think he works there. He pays his room rent here sometimes but he moves around a bit. That's all I know. Please go away."

"He's a student."

"He dropped out."

"Will you look at a photograph, please?"

"No!" The light went out and I was left standing at the door with a photograph in my hand. There was a low hum of insects from the gardens, but otherwise the night was graveyard quiet: there'd be a lot of noise if I tried to force an entry and I didn't imagine the Brisbane cops would be amused at a Sydney private man pushing the citizens around in the wee small hours. I put the photograph away, said goodnight to the door, trying not to sound like a policeman, and left the house.

It was too late to do anything more. I stopped at the first open motel I came to, put crosses at random on the breakfast menu and fell into bed. I lay there with my mind buzzing. "Achieve one thing every day," my Scots grand-mother advised me when I was young. I wondered what she would count as an achievement. I wondered what she would call a day. It was about thirty years and ten thousand days too late to ask her. My mind was hopping, leaping about now: a lifetime could be about twenty-five thousand days. Grandma Kelly had lived to be eighty-odd; had she achieved thirty thousand things? Maybe she had. My one thing—locating Ray Guthrie—didn't seem so much now, but it didn't seem any easier, either. I went to sleep trying to count the things I'd achieved in forty-odd, God-fearing years.

At 5 A.M. it was getting light, and I was wide awake. I stuck my head out the door and sniffed the soft, sub-tropical air. I wrapped one of the motel towels around me and went down to the pool and swam a few laps in the nude. The water was cold and too heavily chlorinated. I stayed under a hot shower for fifteen minutes until I was warm and decontaminated. Then I had an hour to wait for breakfast; I spent some of the time thinking about the information conveyed by the disembodied voice of last night: *other enquirers, moving about, drop-out, voices like cops.* It sounded something like a Brisbane version of the events in Sydney, and wasn't likely to be any more pleasant.

Then I did some thinking about Helen Broadway—time zones; were they any different?—daylight saving and a reasonable hour to call. I ate the soggy breakfast, drank the lukewarm coffee, and made the call. I tried to remember the layout of the flat. No phone by the bed, in the living room; she'd be wearing her silk gown. The phone didn't have to ring for long.

"Christ, long distance," she said. "Where are you—New York?"

"Brisbane. It's eighty degrees already, and I've had a swim."

"I want to see you."

"Me too. Wish you were here."

"Why aren't I?"

"I'm mostly to be found behind the wheel of a car going to places where no one wants to know me. I don't know how long I'll be here. If you left now there's a good chance our paths would cross in mid-air, if you see what I mean."

"I think so. Is your life always so hectic?"

"No, mostly, I have lots of time for Bondi Beach, movies, cappuccino . . ."

"That sounds better. Well, this is costing you something."

"Not me. My client."

"Same man?"

"Yeah. The kid came up to look for his brother. Now we're both looking for him."

"Are-you-in-danger? I say again: Are-you-in-danger?"

I laughed. "Only moderately. I'll call you soon as I get back, Helen."

"Promise?"

I promised, and meant it. I got dressed and paid the bill. The manageress looked at me with disapproval; she almost looked at my credit card with disapproval. Maybe she thought I lowered the tone of the place by being in the pool in the raw.

St. Lucia is a garden suburb and the parts that flank the river would have to be called verdant. Winding roads with smooth footpaths follow the river, and spawn joggers who seemed to outnumber the civilians this fine, crisp morning. I objected to them less now that headbands appeared to be out of fashion. The number of zebra crossings along the river road, controlled by flashing lights, suggested that the joggers had an in with the local council.

The freight yard was a million psychological miles from the certainty and confidence of the big houses by the river and the clear signposts to the university. It was reached by a dusty road that turned off another road which had swung away from the well-heeled section of the district. The railway line here was what the Americans call a spur—an off-shoot, a by-way. There were low, broken-down fences around the goods yard and the road to an old brick office seemed to be marked by smashed wooden freight pallets. A small car park was defined by star stakes which were bent and askew and trailed their wires aimlessly.

I arrived at around 9:30 A.M. which seemed to be too early for commercial activity or civilised communication. The bearded youth in overalls who opened the office door looked at me with loathing.

"What's the matter?" I said.

"You're too early. No one's here."

"Don't put yourself down," I said. "You're here."

He hitched at his overalls, which was unnecessary, because there was no way they could fall down. But he seemed to find it worth doing and he did it again. It dawned on me that he was stoned.

"Let's go inside and talk," I said. He resisted—my second time at being refused entry in ten hours. "Okay, let's stand our ground. Do you know Chris Guthrie?"

He shook his head and hitched the overalls again. It was too much. He's started to shake his head before I'd spoken the name. He was bigger than me and younger, and if he was stoned and I was sober at 9:30 in the morning, that was his problem. I pushed him back against the wall, not gently.

"Guthrie," I barked. "Where?"

He pointed to the right, down the railway track. "He s . . . sometimes sleeps in the old freight car down there. I don't know whether he's there now or not."

I let him come back from the wall and he slid down it into a squatting position. He smiled vacantly up at me.

"I hope nothing important ever happens around here—you wouldn't seem to be up to the job."

"It doesn't," he said.

I tramped down the derelict platform which was only raised a couple of inches above the rail. The whole place was an object lesson in how fast the bush would reclaim the city: the wood I saw was splintered and rotten, the metal was rusted and weeds were pushing up and growing aggressively through the cracked concrete.

The freight car was an old, immobilised ruin, blackened by fire and crumbling from disuse. The sliding door was half-open; it wouldn't budge and I levered myself up and in. Light came in through chinks and gaps in the slatted sides—enough light to see the figure of a man slumped in a corner on a pile of hessian bags.

He was in a half-sitting position with his back against the fire-scorched wall. He was barefoot and wearing jeans and a tattered tee-shirt. A bag hung over one shoulder like half of

87

a poncho. There were a couple of days' worth of youthful fuzz on his face and his brown hair was long and matted: things moved in it. His eyes were closed and his mouth was puffy and blueish. He was Chris Guthrie. The disposable plastic needle hung in his arm like a caterpillar on a leaf. I jerked it out and a trickle of blood ran from the puncture mark which was one of a number, crusted and mottled, running up the inside of his thin, brown arm.

He was wasted and the grime was flaking off him, but there was a slight rise and fall to his chest. I bent forward to lift an eyelid when I heard a sound behind me and spun around. Ray Guthrie was climbing into the freight car; I was temporarily dazzled by the light and against it, Ray looked fuzzy in outline, shaggy like a gorilla. The noise he was making were scarcely more intelligible.

"You bastard," he roared. "Don't touch him."

"Easy, Ray . . ." I moved toward him to conciliate, but I could feel the grim set of my face and with the needle still in my hand I must have looked like the king of the pushers. He jumped at me, arms flailing. I dropped the needle and retreated, trying to keep from stumbling on the debris-strewn floor. He hit me with a long, looping punch that landed on the shoulder and didn't have much sting; I hit back instinctively, catching him on the cheekbone. He went back and I shuffled back to the nearest wall.

"Ray," I gasped, "I'm a friend, your father hired . . ." The word was enough to set him off again; he came in with both fists pumping and it was a matter of protecting myself from damage. I hooked him which brought him up short, then pushed: he stumbled back and fell out of the car. I jumped after him and landed close, but a bit winded. He was game; he pulled himself up and threw another punch. I warded that one off, which takes less wind than throwing one yourself.

"Stop it, Ray. I'm trying to help you."

He bent and picked up a piece from a broken pallet, swung it like a club. I recoiled and that gave him a moment to look at me.

". . . bastard . . . followed us from the pub . . ."

"Right. But . . ."

He threw the wood and I ducked. He ran down the platform, hopping over the uneven surface like a rabbit. I went after him—six paces and I caught my foot and fell. I sprawled on the ground, grazed my hand again and winded myself thoroughly. Lifting my head, I saw him running, jumping, and skittering with terrific speed, down the platform, past the office, and out of the freight yard.

I recovered my breath, picked the dirt out of my palms and went back to the freight car. Chris hadn't moved; his bony chest was still fluttering and there was a thin, reedy sound coming from his throat. I made sure his tongue wasn't going to go down it, and ran back to the office, where the kid with the beard and the personality problem was rolling himself a steadying joint.

"Phone!" I shouted.

He pointed to the floor: the telephone sat on a pile of tattered directories that went back to the Commonwealth Games year and beyond. I swore and fumbled with the mouldy, stuck-together pages. He got his joint going and looked at me with amusement.

"Hospital?" he said.

I nodded and he recited the number. I rang it and got a highly efficient-sounding Emergency service. I told it I needed an ambulance and that I'd better have the police as well while we were at it.

"What's going on, man?"

"It's visiting time," I said. "You've had me and the young bloke who ran past. Now you're going to get the police and an ambulance."

"Shit!" He pinched out the butt and put the inch or so of stained stub in his mouth. "Well, shit. I think there's a train due later this morning."

"That'll make your day," I said.

I ran the rusty water in a tap outside the office, cleaned my face and hands and waited for officialdom.

It came with sirens, flashing lights, starched uniforms, and shiny buttons. The ambulance attendants seemed to think that Chris would pull through. When the cops started on me I doubted if I would make it. They carted me down to a steel and glass tower in the centre of the city which was their headquarters; I wouldn't say they were gentle about it, but at least no one slammed the car door on my fingers. They left me in a bare room ten storys up, and let me look out over their city and think about my sins. The river ran a straight course through the city and then meandered away to the east. I imagined I could see its muddy banks, a malarial plain, a fringe of mangroves where it entered the sea. It put me in a mood to leave Queensland to the Queenslanders— maybe that was the idea.

An Inspector Jervis, who was terse but not overtly hostile, listened to my story after looking at my licence to enquire privately. I told him that I'd been hired to look for Chris Guthrie who'd been out of touch with his family for a worrying period of time. It was close enough to the truth for me to tell it without sweating. He didn't like it much, particularly the reflection it cast on the organisation of which he was a proud member.

"Didn't this Guthrie think we could handle a missing persons case up here, eh?"

Good point, I thought, don't press it. He didn't; I took my cue from Jervis and talked as little as possible. I'd left my gun and burglary tools in the Laser; no one asked me how I was getting around and it seemed like a good thing to keep quiet about. They didn't like me; the only thing they liked about me was my return ticket to Sydney and Jervis suggested I use it, soon.

A phone call to the hospital confirmed the paramedic's impression—Chris was in what they called "shock" from a heroin overdose combined with low physical vitality, but he wasn't in danger. The hospital wanted to know who was going to pay the bills since it was an out-of-state matter. I gave them Paul Guthrie's name and address, which I'd already given to the cops, because it would have been me in the hospital as well if I hadn't

By midday I was on the street again, and by five past in a pub. I had two quick drinks, jostling with counter-lunching policemen. I used the phone in the pub to book a flight back to Sydney and to call a cab to take me back to the freight yard. There was no sign that a train had arrived or ever would again. The hire car had been sitting in the sun for four hours and its vinyl coverings threatened to revert to the original composition of the material. I wound all the windows down and sweltered my way back to Paddington.

The insects were shrill in the overgrown garden and I had to knock very loudly to be heard over the blasting rock music coming from inside the house. Not like the other night—I could kick the door in now and no one would hear. I felt like doing it just on principle; kowtowing to cops isn't my favourite sport. But the noise level dropped and I got the same female voice quavering through the door.

"Yes?"

"Federal police," I shouted.

"What do you want?"

"Open the door, madam, or we'll force it." I thought the "we" was a good touch.

The door opened and a young woman with strained-back hair and a worried mouth looked at me through thick-lensed glasses.

"There's only one of you. I want to see your ID."

I stuck my foot inside the door and gripped its edge. "I'm not a policeman, young lady, although you said I sounded like one the other night."

Her hand flew up to her mouth. "Oh!"

"Yeah, oh. Now I found Chris Guthrie where you suggested—down at the goods yard. He had a needle hanging out of his arm and now he's in the hospital. His father hired me to find him and I'm going to look in his room."

"I'm going to call the police."

"I've just come from them and they wouldn't want to see me again. You can't call from here because there's no phone. By the time you call from outside I'll be gone. Now, why don't you just let me in, and save yourself a lot of bother? You can be back at the books in ten minutes. You call the police and you can forget about studying for today."

She moved aside and let me in.

"Chris's room's through here." I followed her down the passage to a bedroom near the back of the house. The rock music was soft now and the place smelled of incense and coffee. They were good sounds and smells and I let up on the authoritarian manner.

"Nice place," I said. "What're you studying?"

"Politics."

"Always study with the music so loud?"

"Yes, it drowns out the real world."

"Ah. In here?"

She nodded and left me to it. The room was small but well lit from a big window. There was a mattress on the floor with bedding neatly folded on it. A student's desk had books and papers on it and a pen—it looked as if it had been got up from abruptly and never returned to. That was the neat half of the room: on the other side there was a big armchair covered with dirty clothes; there were food scraps balanced on the arms, empty glasses and cans on the floor beside it. There were wadded-up tissues and a bloodstained handkerchief. Between the cushion and the side of the chair I found a plastic cap of a disposable syringe. The room looked as if it had been inhabited by two different people.

I went out, and located the student sitting with a pile of books and notes at the kitchen table. The rock was still soft. She looked up, exasperated.

"I thought you said you'd go?"

"In a minute. What happened to Chris?"

She shrugged. "He went on to drugs."

"Why?"

"I don't know."

"You must know something."

"He went away for a while, a week maybe. When he came back he looked very bad, sick. That's when he started on the stuff. He was only here from time to time—he'd paid some rent in advance."

"He didn't say anything about it?"

"He once said it wasn't his fault, and another time he said he was ashamed of it. But they all say that."

Sympathy wasn't her big thing. I took out the photo of the dark man and held it out for her. "Have you ever seen him?"

"Yes, he was here. I think he's the one who brought Chris in the first time he was sick. He was around a couple of times after that."

"Hear his name?"

"No." She reached out her hand for the knob of the ghettoblaster and I left her to impair her hearing.

11

At the airport I put through a call to Paul Guthrie. I located him at his city office.

"Have you seen Chris?"

"I've seen both of them. Don't be alarmed, but Chris is in the hospital. He's okay." That was stretching it a bit, but a long distance phone call is no way to handle the subtleties. I gave him the details of the hospital and the ward and the businessman in him let me finish. "His mother should come up here, perhaps," I said. "I'll give you the details when I get back to Sydney."

"Who hurt him? How did he get in hospital?"

"He hurt himself, Mr. Guthrie. But he had some help. Ray's in worse shape in some ways. I can't explain now, but he may think his brother's dead. He thinks I'm an enemy and he knows you hired me."

"But Ray's not hurt? Or sick?"

"No, but he's sort of out of control. You'd better take some precautions."

"Ray wouldn't hurt me."

"Maybe not, it's hard to say. If he arrives, just try to keep him calm, and stay calm yourself."

"Do you know what the hell this is all about, Hardy?"

"Not yet. I've got some ideas but not enough information." That was true; it was also true that I was trying to safeguard Pat Guthrie's interests while working for her husband. Tricky.

They were calling my plane and I rang off, still trying to reassure my client. No scanner again. I sat, tightly wedged between a fat man with body odour and a woman who knitted the whole way. I couldn't concentrate on the Hughes book and the clicking of the needles and occasional elbow dig kept me from sleeping.

I thought about the information I had: both brothers had been jerked violently out of their routines and normal habits, and the man I still thought of as "the cop" was involved in the jerking. Ray was stirred up about his real father, but the connection between that and his present wild behaviour was a mystery.

It was a strange case; I'd seen the subject of my enquiries twice but hadn't made any meaningful contact. I had divided my loyalties between my client and his wife. I supposed I'd done some good by getting Chris to the hospital earlier than he would otherwise have made it. It didn't seem like much of an achievement to report to Grandma. Especially with Ray Guthrie thinking of me as an adversary.

The turbulence started about half an hour out of Sydney and intensified as we got closer. The pilot announced that Sydney was being swept by a storm and that we could expect some delays and confusion. I fancied that the body odour got a little worse, but the needles never missed a click.

A summer storm had hit; the gutters and the people had all been caught in light clothes without coats or umbrellas. Those who'd made dashes from the car park or taxis to the terminal looked as if they'd waded there neck-deep. Strangely, everyone seemed to be good humoured about it; the city had had a long dry spell and perhaps the people were ready for the water as well as the plants. I wasn't, myself—the drivers of old cars don't like it.

I drove home cautiously on tyres that would make Jack Brabham weep. I skidded twice and had a heady moment when the wipers hesitated, but I said "mush" to them and they kept going. I parked outside the house and toted my bag up the path through the rain. I was tired from the long day, the traveling and the depressing effect of seeing what heroin can do to a young, healthy man. I wanted a shower and a drink; I wanted to listen to Ella Fitzgerald; I wanted to see Helen Broadway. Instead, I got Frank Parker.

He was sitting halfway up the stairs, which put him about ten metres from the front door and head to head with anyone coming through it. It was a shooting gallery arrangement, with Parker in the shooter's spot—he was in shadow and whoever was in the doorway was beautifully framed against the light. Parker had a gun in his hand and he was ready to shoot.

"Jesus, Frank!" I dropped the bag and was almost alarmed enough to try putting up my hands. Parker stretched his long legs in front of him and stood up just a couple of steps above the floor. He came down the steps, favouring his left side. He lowered the gun to his side; I closed the door behind me and we met halfway up the passage.

"The dentist let me in," he said. "Must be handy for a bloke in your game and with your personality to have someone around who can fix your teeth."

"Put the bloody gun away." I went past him toward the kitchen and the fridge. "How long have you been here?"

"Since last night."

"Sorry I didn't change the sheets." He didn't say anything to that and I didn't find out why until later. "I need a drink."

He followed me through to the kitchen, where I decided that wine wasn't the answer. I got the whisky out of the cupboard where it usually lives a lonely life, grabbed a glass and poured a short one. "Cheers." I put it down, took a deep breath and looked at him.

He had a rumpled look which was unusual for him and he'd missed a shave; for a man with a beard as heavy as his that's like missing two shaves. He set the safety on the revolver with his thumb and put it on the table. I held up the bottle and he nodded. I poured one for him and another for me.

"What's up, Frank?"

He sipped the scotch and made a face. "Not very good."

"None of it's any good when you come right down to it. Did I ask what was up?"

I pushed aside the books and magazines on the table to make eating and drinking room the way I always had to. We sat down, Parker carefully, protecting the left side. He had a preoccupied, almost embarrassed look. He was a very private, self-contained man and the situation wasn't an easy one for him. I gave him time. The window was still wet from the rain and the afternoon sun coming through broke up into pin-points of light. I drank some more of the cut-price scotch.

"I got a bit busy after we finished the other day," Parker said. "Came into town and poked around. Here and there. I was really trying to sort out my own thing—who might have set me up." He sipped his drink and rubbed his chin as if he could feel the whiskers growing. "But I made a few discreet enquiries about your matter too, especially about him." He got the photograph out of his shirt pocket and laid it on the table. "Strange thing is, it looks like your problem and mine are related."

"You know who he is." I was excited, feeling for the breakthrough.

"Yeah. I thought he was familiar but it wouldn't click. A

97

former colleague clinched it for me. He's a bloke named Henry Hayes; they call him 'Bully.' "

"I'll trump you," I said. "He's a Queensland cop."

He nodded. "He was. He acts as if he still is. He's bad news; a hit man, basically. He killed six men officially in the line of duty and a few more unofficially. He left the force early this year."

"Why? Kicked out?"

"No. They couldn't kick him out. Knows too much dirt. He's said to have the goods on top men in the force and sideways—on the politicians and the crims. He's invulnerable."

"Or highly dispensable."

He shook his head. "Not so far. Like I said, he acts as if he's still a cop—he exerts the authority without the responsibility."

We both drank, but I didn't taste mine. We were probably thinking the same thing—that a rogue policeman with high-level backing and protection was about as dangerous an animal as there was.

"So why did he quit? Why not go on killing people and drawing his pay?"

"No ones knows. But it's something very big. I do know it involves Liam Catchpole and Dottie Williams."

"They're not big time."

"They are now. Look, I've narrowed down the things I was working on that could've been a big threat to anyone of three."

"That all? I can only do one thing at a time."

"Luxury. Yeah, three, that's disregarding old stuff. I felt I was getting close to whoever killed the heroin courier at Mascot. You read about that?"

I nodded.

"I had a customs bloke ready to talk. I thought I was getting warm on the judge who got bombed. His daughter died and her boyfriend was sweating his guts out over it. Really pushing. He had a lawyer over a barrel and was getting some names. Bad stuff goes on in those courts. And there's a bloke in Parramatta, coming out soon, who I was keeping under wraps. He won't be pleased that I got the push."

"Why? What's his game?"

"D'you remember Collinson, the one who killed his partner and took off with the money?"

"Yeah, think so."

"Wasn't all that much fuss about it. My man had some information about an accomplice who didn't want to go on being an accomplice. It was going to take careful handling."

"I'm glad I'm not in law enforcement. How much money was involved in that Collinson thing again?" I finished my drink and poured just a whisper more.

"About six million. Easy on that, Cliff. We've got things to do." He touched his side and winced.

"What happened to you?"

"Someone made a pass at me—with a knife, in Crown Street."

I whistled. "Is it bad?"

"Big scratch. The dentist fixed it." He smiled and I began to get the idea.

"Where's Hilde now?"

"She went off to do the disgusting things she does. She'll be back. Very competent young woman."

"Yeah. She is. Look, Frank; I'm glad you felt you could come here and all, but you've left a lot of things hanging. What's the connection between your thing and mine? And why *are* you here?" I felt like finishing my whisky but something about his face made me give up the idea.

He leaned forward across the table. "Here's the connection. I think those earlier goes at me were just warnings, but this one," he touched his ribs again, "was the real thing. And it happened shortly after I made the enquiry and got the answers about Hayes. There was time for the word to pass and my feeling is that's what happened. Why'm I here? I went home and there was a three man crew watching the house. Someone's getting serious."

"Wasn't Hayes himself, was it? At your place?"

"I doubt it. He's said to be very good at what he does. These three weren't very good."

"So what do you want to do now?"

"Who would you say was the softest out of Catchpole, Spotswood, and Williams?"

I thought about it. "I don't know all that much about them."

"I do," Frank said. "I've been asking."

"None of them's soft, but I'd say Spotswood if I had to pick one."

"You're right. He's the one. Well, we have to figure out a way to get hold of him and scare the living shit out of him." He banged his fist on the table. "I'm buggered if I'm going to be hunted by an animal like Hayes. I'm going hunting myself. What do you say?"

"Yes. Tonight?"

"Tonight."

12

I phoned Guthrie again. He told me his wife had flown to Brisbane to see her son.

"Drugs, they said." His voice seemed to handle the word with difficulty.

"That's right. But he couldn't have been using them for very long. When did you last see him?"

"Six months," he said dully.

"So it's a good deal less than that. He'll get over it. Could be a lot worse."

"But what the hell is happening to my family! He was a student! At university! Now I hear they call him a labourer or something—I just don't understand. What happened?"

"He was under some kind of pressure. I don't know why yet. I'm still working on it. I hope to get some answers soon. Any sign of Ray yet?"

"No. Do you need any more money?"

"Not so far. How's your wife?"

"Bloody strange. She seemed almost glad to get the news from Brisbane. No, I don't mean that. She jumped at the idea of going up there, almost seemed she wanted to get away from me as much as see Chris."

"Just glad to have something to do, probably," I lied. "Just sit tight, Mr. Guthrie. I know it's hard, but it's all you can do. All I can tell you now is that I'm going to put on some pressure myself—on the Catchpole crowd."

"That sounds like the right idea. Wish I could help."

"Be there. Be there for Ray and Chris and your wife."

"Makes me feel old," he grumbled. He was active by nature, sensitive enough to know his limitations but energetic enough to chafe under them. All I could do was throw him a bone.

"If you can do anything, like some driving or something like that, I'll get on to you."

"Thanks, Hardy. Appreciate it. The Northbridge place feels like a barn with only me in it. We've got a flat at the Double Bay marina. I'll stay there until Pat gets back. You've got the number?"

I checked, told him I had it, reassured him again, and hung up. I had a mental picture of him sitting by the phone, which I didn't like too much—it could be a long sit.

Hilde came home and made coffee. I gave her and Frank some time on their own, and when I rejoined them for the drink they seemed to have spent it well. Hilde passed Frank his coffee and gave his bristles a rub.

"Just like a Hun," I said, "knuckling under to authority."

She smiled at me. "Get stuffed, Cliff. How's it going with the one with the sexy voice?"

I grunted. "It'd go all right if I wasn't spending so much time with coppers."

"They're not so bad." She ran her hand over the bristles again, almost as if she was just interested in the texture. Almost.

"This is a conspiracy, Frank, you know that," I said.

Parker nodded.

"What is?" Hilde said.

I filled her in on what was happening, partly to hear myself review it and partly because Hilde sometimes has a sensible suggestion to make. Sometimes she has a brilliant suggestion to make. But not this time.

"You go out on a limb doing that, Frank," she said.

"I'm on the limb already. I haven't got anything to lose."

"It's all right for Cliff," she persisted. "He hasn't got a reputation to worry about."

"A policeman hasn't got a reputation either," Parker said. His voice was bitter-edged, impatient. "He's got his job or he hasn't got it. That's all."

"Touched as I am by Hilde's assessment of my character," I said, "we can all do without the vocational philosophy. What bloody reputation does a dentist have anyway?"

She flared up. "I'm a dental *researcher!* And you'd have some reputation if you weren't so dumb! If you stopped running around at all hours of the day and night . . . being bashed up."

"How would I make a living?"

"You're *not* dumb. You could be a crime reporter or a crime . . . writer or something . . ."

Parker burst out laughing and broke the tension. "Hardy! He couldn't be a writer! I've read one of his voluntary statements—no one believed it."

"Poetic licence," I said. "You should read my reports to clients. I'll show you one, Hilde—I reckon you'd say I should stick to being bashed."

She was still ruffled but the edge was off the moment. We drank some of her very good coffee, and talked about nothing for a while until I got us back on course.

"How do we grab Spotswood?"

Hilde broke some conciliatory eggs into a bowl. She looked at Parker. "Where does he live?"

"Where does he drink?" I said.

Parker had the answer to that question and to a few others. I knew a bit about Catchpole and Spotswood myself because of their connections with Glebe, but Parker had done some deep spadework. The "Tiny" nickname for Spotswood was ironic. When I'd last seen him there must have been sixteen stone on his six foot four frame and there were no signs that he was interested in dieting. He used to hang around Glebe in the days before the professional classes moved in. Back then, when the freeway was scheduled to go through a thousand bedrooms, and the banks wouldn't lend on anything closer to the city than Haberfield, almost every street in Glebe had at least one boarding house and there was a drifting population of people who had reasons to drift.

In those days Tiny Spotswood drank at the Toxteth, bet at Harold Park, and exercised his prostate in the place above the barber's shop in Ross Street. He'd done some boxing in the 1960s and Liam Catchpole and been his manager. Boxing was dying then and people like Spotswood and Catchpole were part of the reason why. When Tiny had taken all the falls on TV and in the clubs anyone could stomach, Catchpole managed a liquor store in which you couldn't have found an order form or an invoice if you searched for a month. Tiny's job was loading and unloading the trucks, being around when restaurant and bar owners showed a lack of interest in being supplied by Liam and generally kicking when he was told to kick.

Most of that was before my time in Glebe, although I did arrive before the middle class invasion that changed everything. The boarding houses got changed back into family residences and trees started sprouting everywhere. The mortgage-holders objected to the twenty-four hour clink of bottles and rattle of trucks around Catchpole's premises—they seemed to think it was worse than the sound of their renovating, even at the weekends. Once-firm understandings broke down and Spotswood got a couple of years for grievous bodily harm. Catchpole moved away. No loss. He and Tiny would have been genuinely shocked by the new power blocs like the Lesbian Mothers Against Rape, anyway.

I couldn't imagine Spotswood moving to Mount Druitt though, and when Parker told me that he drank at the Crimea in Rozelle I wasn't surprised. If you ignore Annandale and Lilyfield, Rozelle is just next door to Glebe, really.

The roads were still very wet as Frank and I drove to Rozelle with Hilde's omelette and coffee inside us. Frank had left his car in Harbord and we were in the Falcon. I showed him the gun clip under the dashboard.

"I think that's illegal. Aren't you restricted to carrying your gun on the left-hand side with a cork up the barrel?"

"Something like that. Can we be sure Tiny'll be there tonight?"

"My information is that he lives there."

"Lives in a pub?"

"Yeah. Do you know the Crimea?"

"I know it. I'm not sure I'd even drink in it by choice, let alone live there."

"I'm glad you changed out of those poncy shoes then."

"They're no good for stomping on fingers. So what's Tiny doing these days? Besides helping Liam Catchpole help the authorities with their enquiries?"

The look he gave me wasn't friendly. "Where'd you be if nobody told you anything?"

"Stuffed."

"Right."

Not even the cheekiest of real estate sharks would describe the part of Rozelle graced by the Crimea Hotel as "will suit Balmain buyers." Narrowness is the theme; narrow streets, narrow houses, narrow shopfronts. The section is hilly and the streets run at odd angles but the effect is crippled rather than quaint. The pub, which faces a cramped football ground notorious for its bogginess in winter, juts out awkwardly on a corner, forming a crazy, erratic building line. The dominant colour is dirty grey, and the part of the upper level which hangs over the street looks too heavy for the narrow posts that support it. We parked near the football field pointing in the direction which I thought would get me fairly directly to Victoria Road—in the maze of small streets it'd be hard to be sure.

I had a shirt out over my pants again and Parker watched me sourly as I tucked the gun away behind.

"Where's yours?" I said.

"Under here," he tapped his undamaged side, up near the armpit. He was wearing a light poplin zip-jacket and a clean white shirt of mine. At risk to its motor, I'd lent him my shaver and he had his beard down to a flat blueness. "I hope we don't need the bloody things," he said.

"Has Tiny got any guts?"

We stepped clear of the car. "Opinions differ," Frank said. It reminded me of the meaningless, pointless chatter we used to fall into in Malaya before we went in to some place where people were likely to shoot at us. It covered nervousness, or was supposed to. I didn't like to be reminded of those feelings.

"What else do we know about him?"

Parker adjusted the zip on his jacket. "He's a boxing freak—knows who KO'd who where and in what round— all that crap."

I stopped. "Have you got any ideas on how we're going to get him out of the pub, if he's there?"

"No. My side is hurting. I'm getting involved with your housemate. I'm confused. I'm too angry for good ideas, or any ideas."

106

"Here's one. The Boxing Commission's sitting."

"So what?"

"I could spin Tiny a story about him giving evidence to one of the Commissioners. That could be you, in the car."

"Why'm I in the car?"

"I'm sorry, Frank. But you look like a cop and you move like a cop."

"No, I mean why am I in the car if I'm a Boxing Commissioner?"

" 'Cause he's got a criminal record."

"Can't they talk to crims?"

"I don't know. Tiny wouldn't know. It might work. If we can just get him out, we're in business."

"I don't . . ."

I handed him my gun and tucked my shirt in. "Let's give it a try. If I get in trouble I'll yell, and you can come and be a cop. You'll have two guns, you can be as angry as you like."

He didn't care for it but he agreed. I watched him walk back to the car and climb in. He settled himself in the passenger seat and gave me the nod. In his clean shirt and light jacket and with his severe profile he looked the part. The Falcon wasn't too impressive, but it was parked in the shadows and if Tiny was hooked a detail like that wouldn't unhook him.

I went into the bar pulling out my money as I entered. It was small and hot on the mild night although it looked like the sort of place that would be an ice box in winter. Now the smoke was thick and the beer fumes drifted with the draughts from the open windows and doors. There were about a dozen men sitting around the three-sided bar; the Crimea didn't offer anything like pool, tables and chairs, or barmaids. It was a man-to-man, middy-to-middy blood-house.

Tiny Spotswood was part of a group sitting along one of the short sides of the bar. He had a wall behind him to lean his bulk against. He'd expanded since I'd last seen him, and all around the equator. He must have weighed eighteen stone and the schooner he was working on now would be one in a very long chain. A good length of zipper showed at the top of his pants where they failed to accommodate his belly. The Hawaiian print shirt he was wearing showed sunsets and palm trees for a holiday resort.

Spotswood and the two nearest him were talking about racehorses, not boxing. It would have been too much to ask to walk into the middle of a bet on whether Dave Sands was ever stopped. I ordered a beer and positioned myself as close to the punting discussion as I could. I was a stranger and therefore intrusive, but they were a tolerant mob, especially as I didn't have my Italian shoes on.

The man closest to Tiny up-ended his schooner and pulled out of the school.

"Gotta get home," he said.

"Under the thumb, Bert?" Spotswood jeered. His fleshy face under the thin, gingery hair was loose and unco-ordinated, glistening with sweat. He was very drunk. The retirer shook his head.

"Haven't got your liver, Tiny."

Spotswood stuck a cigarette in his face and laughed around it, just managing to keep the cigarette in place. "Haven't got a fuckin' liver," he roared. "Haven't had one for fuckin' years."

That got him a laugh. There was a space to move into now and there was no point in being shy. I got out a card that said: "Michael Simmonds—Consultant" and flashed it in front of Tiny's bleary eyes.

"Excuse me, Mr. Spotswood. I'm Mike Simmonds— from the Department of Sport and Recreation."

"What's that, mate?"

"The New South Wales Government—Department of Sport and Recreation. Can I buy you a drink?"

"Why not?" He waved to the barman. "Cec, the Government's buying me a bloody schooner."

The other drinker from the group edged away. "Don't go away, mate," I said. "You might be able to help, too."

"Help, how?" Spotswood looked at me with a mixture of drunken scorn and caution. His schooner came and he took a big pull on it. I drank some of my beer and the other man looked at us with sceptical curiosity. The rest of the bar went about its business.

"I'm told you're an expert on boxing," I said.

"Boxing. Yeah, I know a bit."

"You know there's an enquiry going on at the moment?"

"Fuckin' wowsers and poofters!" Spotswood's face flushed; the heightened colour gave him an over-ripe, ready-to-burst look. "Boxing's a good sport, right, Phil?"

Phil nodded and sipped his schooner. "Usta be."

"Could be again, if they'd leave it alone and give it a bit 'a publicity. Fuckin' good fights in the clubs but do you ever see a fuckin' word about 'em in the bloody papers?"

"You never do, no," Phil said.

"There's still public interest?" I asked.

"Man's bloody game. They should ban the bloody women like they did in the old days. Then there'd be some fuckin' goes."

I leaned closer to him. "That's a very interesting point of view. That's original. Would you be willing to give evidence to the Commission. I must say all the evidence so far is going the other way . . ."

"They gonna bloody ban it?" Spotswood took a belligerent swig.

"They could, unless there's something said on the other side. The doctors are opposed, the churches . . ."

"What would they fuckin' know? Need to talk to a man been in it!" He pushed his face close to mine and I waited for my eyes to water from the beer fumes. "I had thirty-three fuckin' fights!"

"How many'd you win, Tiny?" asked Phil, who was just possibly a wag.

"Never mind. More'n I lost. 's not winnin', 's bein' there! Know all about it. What's a man gotta do? Go 'n talk to some cunt in Parliament?"

"No, no," I said quickly. "Matter of fact, one of the Commissioner's in my car outside. Mr. Groves. He's anxious to talk to you."

He thumped his meaty fist on the bar. "Bring 'im in! Buy 'im a drink!"

"No, he can't approach you."

"Why not?"

"Don't be offended, Mr. Spotswood, but it's a matter of your criminal record. But Mr. Groves himself isn't preju-diced; he wants to get the truth about boxing from all angles. Between you and me, I think he's the only Commissioner with an open mind. I'm aware, and I'm sure you're aware, that there are interested parties who'd be grateful to you if you could put the sort of case you've been making here to one of the Commissioners. It wouldn't have to be in public hearings. The word would get around if you know what I mean. Would you come and have a word with Mr. Groves? I promise you you won't be sorry."

"Awright." He heaved his swollen body off the stool and stood swaying for a moment, getting his balance. "Back in a minute, Phil."

Phil nodded and Spotswood lumbered towards the door; I walked behind him wishing we'd dug a bear trap by the car, and had a block and tackle to lift him out and a King Kong cage to keep him in.

"Where is he?" He stood on the footpath hitching at his sagging waistband. I hoped he wouldn't try to lean against one of the slender posts.

"Over there." I pointed to the car. Parker appeared to be making entries in a notebook. He wasn't looking our way but I had the feeling he knew just what was going on. Spotswood walked slowly toward the car and I kept right behind him, chattering.

"You know, Mr. Spotswood, I heard some blokes having an interesting bet about Dave Sands."

"Bloody gentleman," Spotswood rumbled.

"Yes, now the question was whether he was ever knocked out or not."

We reached the car.

"Dave was never stopped," he said; he leaned on the car for support.

"Mr. Groves, this is Mr. Spotswood." Parker used his notebook like a conjurer's handkerchief; he dropped it and as Spotswood's eyes followed it he passed my gun to me through the open window and brought his own up to within a few inches of the big man's nose.

"Hello, Tiny," he said.

I rammed my .38 into Tiny's back, through the flab into the place where what was left of his kidneys would be. He moved away from it and closer to the car and to Parker's gun.

"What's this?"

"It's what it looks like, Tiny. You've seen it before. Now get in the back or I'll put one in your kidneys. Your choice."

Parker reached over and opened the back door from inside. Spotswood hesitated, perhaps considering a yell to the pub. I discouraged that by jabbing him again; he moved toward the door and I eased the gun away so he wouldn't know where it was. But he was too drunk for any swift moves and he probably knew it. He bent and stumbled into the back seat. I followed and dragged the door shut. Parker started the car.

"Easy?" he said.

"Pretty easy. Follow this, takes you to Victoria Road, I think."

Spotswood leaned back against the seat; with his body relaxed he spread over nearly half of it, there'd be no athletic door-openings and divings-out for Tiny. A sweet, sickly smell—beer, sweat, and fear—rose from him. Parker drove cautiously, getting the feel of the car.

"Okay?" I said. I meant the car.

"Yeah. We've got a problem—I originally thought we'd do it at your dump."

"I thought you might."

"But with Hilda there I don't like the idea."

"Hilde."

"I call her Hilda, like it better. Have you got any ideas?"

I thought about it, weighed it up, and decided. "Yes. I know where we can go."

Tiny tensed up beside me. "Me bladder's full, I have trouble with it . . ."

"That's tough," I said. "And you were wrong, Tiny. Yolande Pompey stopped Dave in the seventh in London in 1951."

13

We didn't talk any more. It's not the way to do it. Even with an ox like Tiny Spotswood, the real intimidation is a matter of what happens in the subject's imagination, not outside threats.

Parker had a grim, unrelenting driving style; he sat straight whatever the car was doing, which is the way they teach cops to drive. There was something frightening about his mobility, watching it from behind, so that I was beginning to get apprehensive about what was coming up myself. Not as much as Spotswood though. The smell came off him more and more strongly and his voice seemed to go up an octave. He wriggled.

"I've got to piss!"

I didn't say anything.

Guthrie's marina at Double Bay looked squat and forbidding. The high mounted lights and some barbed wire running along the top of one section of fence gave it a Stalag 17 look.

The water was dark and still; the boats ground and clanked at their moorings and only a few were showing lights. There were no wild parties going on, no strolling couples, no yachtsman comfortingly smoking a cigarette on his deck. Parker took the Falcon down a concrete ramp to the marina office, which was closed. There were lights showing in a box-like structure up on the roof of the office building. Parker tapped the horn and Paul Guthrie's face, pale and agitated, appeared at the window. Parker turned around and held his gun on Tiny while I got out. I stood in the headlights of the car and let Guthrie see me.

"No names," I said. "How do we get up there?"

He pointed into the shadows and, by straining my eyes, I could see a metal ladder running up the side of the building to the roof. Ten metres or a bit more, a couple of dozen rungs. Eighteen-stone Tiny Spotswood was going to love this.

We hauled him out of the car and prodded him across to the ladder; he baulked at it, but a look at Parker's hawkish face and the way he handled his .45 automatic changed his mind. I went up first and it was a stiff climb for the leg muscles; I waited at the top on the flat roof with my heart rate raised and a feeling of distaste for what we were doing. Spotswood's foot slipped a couple of rungs up and he swore; he kept swearing as he came up, rung by rung, slowly, and breathing as if it was a one-in-two sand dune. Parker came up quickly behind him, and we moved quietly over the roof to where Guthrie held the door of his flat open.

From the elevation, I could see down on the moorings; the lighting on the walkways was widely spaced and there were long areas of deep shadow. There were gaps in the ranks of moored boats, and one section of jetty at which there were none at all. I looked across the water to where Roberta Landy-Drake would be doing her evening's drinking, but that only made me think of Helen and it was no time for that.

The three of us filed past Guthrie in silence; he was wearing a tracksuit and had one of his boating books in his hand. His hair was spiky and rumpled again. I brought up the rear and closed the door.

"Spotswood," I said. "I have to talk to him, and you know why."

114

Guthrie nodded.

I made sure that Tiny couldn't see my wink. "I want you to go and get a small motor boat or a dinghy or something and bring it to the closest point to here. Put plenty of rope in it and something heavy—metal, you know what I mean."

"Yes."

"Will I be able to see you from in here?"

"Yes."

"Okay. Take your time."

I took the book from him and he went out. Tiny heard all this and his huge belly sagged. Then he swore and the urine soaked his trouser leg. Parker jerked his head and Tiny shuffled into the flat. We went through to a small room with a big window looking out over the water. There was a couch and a couple of armchairs by the window, a kitchenette at the end of the room and a door through to a bedroom. I gathered up a newspaper and spread the sheets thickly in one of the chairs. Spotswood got the idea. When he was settled in the chair, Parker sat opposite him on the couch and didn't say anything.

I went to the kitchenette, looking for a drink. Guthrie had a few cans of light beer in the fridge; I held one up to Parker who shook his head. I opened one for myself and poured some into a plastic mug I found on the sink. I came over and handed the mug to Tiny.

"You can have yours in a plastic cup because you wet your pants." He took the mug and drank it down in one go—he'd have done the same whether it was overproof rum or elderberry wine. I took the cup away and sipped my can.

"What do youse want?" His voice was a high register croak.

"It's pretty simple, Tiny," Parker said. "You tell us what Liam Catchpole and 'Bully' Hayes are up to, or we'll kill you."

"Oh, Jesus."

"No help there," I said. "If you tell us we won't kill you. Of course, if Liam and Hayes knew you talked to us *they'd* kill you. You're stuffed either way, but we'll give you some protection against 'Bully,' or at least time to shoot through."

"What's all that shit with the little guy—about the boat?"

"That little guy is Mr. Boats. He knows the currents, the deep water—the lot. Out there even a big, fat slob like you will just vanish if you do it right."

"Let me go to the toilet."

"No," Parker said. "Don't waste our time, Tiny. If you don't tell us we'll just tidy you up and go about it another way."

The way he said it made me wonder whether Parker had ever done this sort of thing before and if he really meant it. Tiny caught the same note in the words but there was some hardness and defiance left in him, as well as the fear.

"Bullshit."

"Have it your own way." Parker gestured to me. "Is he there yet?"

I looked out the window. Guthrie was sitting in a dinghy with a big Thompson outboard attached. He was only about fifteen metres from where I stood and I could see two big coils of rope and a heavy metal grill—like the cover of a street drain—in the boat with him.

"He's there," I said.

"Right." Parker grabbed the front of Tiny's shirt and ripped a section out of it. He wadded it up and motioned Spotswood to stand. When he was up Parker chopped him savagely on the side of the neck; Tiny's mouth opened to yell and Parker rammed the material into it. He twisted his fat arm up behind him and rammed him in the spine with his gun. Spotswood moved stiffly the way Parker turned him.

116

We all stood at the window and looked down on Guthrie. He was wearing a knitted cap on his head, pulled down low and in his dark tracksuit and with the oars resting easily across his legs he looked like the man for the job. His tired, worry-filled eyes looked up at us emptily. Spotswood shook his head violently and tore the gag out with his free hand.

"All right, all right, I'll tell you what I know." He tried to turn around, but Parker kept him the way he was, looking down at the boat in the water. "Well, 'Bully,' he's from Queensland, and . . ."

"We don't want the bloody encyclopaedia," Parker snarled, "and I know enough about it to tell if you're lying. I'll make it easier for you. Who is Hayes supposed to hit?"

"Collinson."

I opened my mouth but Parker motioned me to shut it. "In Australia, is he?"

"Yeah."

I waved down to Guthrie to indicate that he could finish the charade with the boat—if that was what it had been. I gave him a thumbs up, too. Parker eased back on Tiny and let him come around and sit down again. I gave him the half-full can of beer and he drained it.

"What're Liam and Dottie doing?"

"They're helping 'Bully' flush this Collinson."

Parker and I both spoke at once; I backed off and let him in first.

"What d'you know about a cop named Parker?"

"Bugger all. I heard he was getting close to Collinson and people wanted him stopped. That's all."

It was my turn. "The Guthrie kid, where's he fit in?"

"He's Collinson's kid. Hayes found that out somehow. Liam's been trying to use him to get to Collinson. The kid's fuckin' Dottie; he's been on some jobs. Liam's working on him."

117

"How do you mean?"

"Look, I don't fuckin' know, do I? They reckon on using the kid to get to Collinson. I dunno how."

"What about the other Guthrie kid—the one in Brisbane?"

"Don't know nothin' about that. Could I have another drink? Shit, that's all I know."

I got out the photograph of the man I knew as Peter Keegan and showed it to Spotswood.

"Is this Collinson?"

The question itself seemed to alarm him and he looked at the picture as if he was staring into the face of the gorgon. "Jesus," he breathed. "I dunno. But if it is what you've got there's worth a fuckin' mint. There's no pictures of Collinson—none at all."

"That's right," Parker said. "Let's have a look at that. You watch Tiny in case he decides he's bullet-proof."

I watched him but there didn't seem to be much point in it. His mind was on other things and other places. I went back to the fridge and opened another can.

"You got a name to go with this?" Parker said.

"Yeah . . ."

"Keep it to yourself for now. We've got the connection between your business and mine, though."

"Looks that way—but it's getting complicated. I'll need to think it out."

"We'll have to park Tiny somewhere," Parker said. "Any ideas?"

"Whaddya mean?" Spotswood yelped. "I told youse what I know. I won't talk to nobody!"

"I know you mean well, Tiny," I said. "But you're dumb and Liam isn't. He'd have it out of you in no time. You wouldn't have time to get your first schooner down."

"No."

118

"Yes." Parker handed me back the photo and looked at Tiny as if he was wrapping around a parcel—something to discard. "Let's go and have a talk to your Mr. Boats, he might have some ideas."

I doubted that and reluctant wasn't the word for Tiny, but Parker had a hardness to him that carried all before it. We went out of the flat. Nails had lifted on the surface of the roof, and we had to pick up our feet. We went across to the top of the ladder, and Parker motioned me to go first. I turned, went down backwards and was half-way when I heard the shout and the high-pitched scream. I flattened myself to the ladder, braced and gripped hard, as Spotswood's body flopped heavily past me. My face was digging into the wall when he hit the cement with a noise like wood splitting I went down fast and heard Parker coming after me.

Tiny was lying face up; there was brain pulp on the cement; blood and other matter. His eyes were open and his jaw hung slackly like Jess Willard's after Dempsey finished with him at Toledo. I noticed that he had only a dozen or so teeth in his head. The big body was spread out and relaxed; the urine stain was a wide, dark stripe down the inside of his trouser legs.

"What happened?" I said.

Parker stood beside me; his skin was pale under the blue beard and his mouth was drawn into a hard line. "Caught his foot on one of the nails, he bloody near took me with him. Shit, this is a mess!" He patted his pocket, feeling for the cigarettes he no longer used. "Not that he was any bloody loss. He saw a few off himself."

I stared at him, wondering. But it didn't seem like the sort of thing Parker would do. To the law though, it wouldn't make much difference—by abducting Spotswood we'd put ourselves in jeopardy.

"What's this Guthrie like?" Parker snapped.

"You saw him. He's good. This is bad, Frank."

"It could be worse; he was drunk, he fell, he's dead. Who's going to care? You reckon Guthrie could sit pat?"

Paul Guthrie had asked for action and now he had his share; I was sure he wanted to see the whole thing through. This was pretty rough, but I remembered his anguish at his perception that his family was under threat.

"I think I can square him," I said. "But I'm going to have to let him in on a few things. I'll also have to tell him who you are."

"Here he comes," Parker said. "Go ahead."

Down the walkway, Guthrie was hurrying out of the shadows towards us.

"Listen," Parker hissed. "You can't tell him about Collinson. I want to flush him out as much as 'Bully' Hayes does."

14

Guthrie looked down at Tiny Spotswood's body. He swallowed hard, pulled off the knitted cap, and ran his hand through his hair.

"He fell," I said. "I'm sorry to involve you in this, Mr. Guthrie."

"I asked you to," he said. "Did this man have anything to do with what happened to Ray and Chris?"

"Not directly. I can't say that. But the people he's associated with are at the centre of it. He knew something about it." I turned towards Parker. "This is Frank Parker, Mr. Guthrie. He's after Catchpole for a different reason. Our paths have sort of crossed."

Parker and Guthrie nodded at each other, warily.

"We're going to have to ask you for more help, Mr. Guthrie," Parker said quietly. "Looks very quiet tonight. Is anyone likely to have seen us here?"

Guthrie shook his head. "No, very dead tonight." He suddenly heard what he'd said and looked down at the corpse again. He clamped his jaw tight and looked up at me. "What do you want me to do?"

"Something pretty hard," Parker said. "Just do nothing. If someone finds him tonight, just act as you would if you'd never seen him or us. If it works out that you find him in the morning, just do the same. You don't know anything. Can you do it?"

Guthrie looked at Parker as if he was a horse in the

yearling ring. He grabbed my arm and moved me away. "Hang on, I want a private word with Hardy."

He drew me away into the shadows.

"Who is he?"

"He's a cop. Or was. This Catchpole business has cost him his job and his reputation. He's out to get Catchpole and some others. He's a good cop—and an honest one."

Guthrie pondered it, then nodded. "That'll do me. If you say he's okay I'll take a chance on him."

"It doesn't have to be a life-long pledge. If things got really sticky for you, of course you could talk freely—and we'd back you up. But we need some time now, and some secrecy. A session down at police headquarters could blow the whole thing."

"Why?"

"Not secure."

"You can't trust the police?"

"Hard to—not all of them, anyway. I trust Parker, though."

"Your job is to protect my boy. Is that the way you see it?"

"Yes."

"You know, Hardy, a few months ago I would have described myself as the happiest man in Sydney. Now, I feel my life is turning to shit. My boys . . . Pat going off like that. A man with his brains all over my . . . Turning to shit. I'm hoping to pull something out of it, though. I won't get it all back, I know that. But I want to salvage something. Do you think I've got a chance?"

I thought of Pat Guthrie's graceful walk, the sea poems on Ray's spick-and-span boat, the neat, purposeful half of Chris's room. Those things felt solid, despite all the surrounding disarray. "Yes," I said, "I think you've got a good chance."

"Protect my boy. I'll back you up here. Don't worry."

Parker was looking edgy while this was going on. Guthrie moved resolutely back towards him. I nodded to Parker and he and Guthrie exchanged respectful nods.

We asked Guthrie to remove any traces of our presence in the flat. I suggested that he might care to go up to Queensland soon and he said he'd think about it. He turned away from us and from the broken thing on the cement, and climbed the ladder. He went up easily, sure-footed and neat in his movements. Parker and I watched him until we heard the door to the flat close. Parker let out a slow breath that whistled through his teeth.

"What did you tell him?"

"Relax, Frank. I didn't even hint that you want to use his kid for bait."

We both showed the strain on the drive back to Glebe. I was feeling some relief, some apprehension at the conflict coming up between us, some guilt. *Why would he tell me not to name names in front of Spotswood if he meant to knock him off?* I thought. There was some comfort in that.

I drove badly, skidding on the wet roads and misjudging the turns. Parker was sitting stiffly; he swore when I hit a pothole.

"Sorry," I said.

He didn't speak, but took his hand out of his jacket pocket with the piece of Spotswood's shirt he'd used as a gag in it. I looked quickly sideways at him; he was chewing at his lower lip, really digging the teeth in.

"Come on, Frank. You've seen it before."

"Yeah, I've seen it before. I've seen them pushed—I'm wondering if there's any difference."

It was late when we got back, but Hilde was still up, waiting for Frank. She gave him a kiss and he grabbed and hugged her and they nuzzled each other without caring whether I was there taking pictures or not. I left them in the front of the house and went to make coffee and get out the scotch, what there was left of it.

Hilde came out first and stood in the doorway; she was wearing a white overall and a red tee-shirt; her pale face was slightly pink where it had been rubbed by Frank's beard.

"What kind of a session is this going to be, stone-face?" she said.

"A hard one."

"I think I'll go to bed."

"If we need the woman's point of view we'll call you."

She came into the kitchen, stepped up and kissed me on the cheek—my first such salute from her, or maybe the second. There were no smells of oily water, stale urine, and death about her; she smelled of shampoo and toothpaste. "Don't be a shit, Cliff," she said. "It doesn't suit you."

She went out and they did some wrestling on the stairs; then Parker walked in, looking like a policeman. He took in my coffee-making sourly, pulled out the piece of cloth, went across to the sink and burnt it. The dark wisp of smoke curled up to the roof like a votive offering.

"Sit down, Frank, and have a drink. We've got a problem—call it a conflict of interests."

He lowered himself into a chair and stuck out his long legs—they stretched halfway across the kitchen. I poured the coffee and we both added some whisky to our cups.

"Keegan," I said. "I know the soldier in the photo as Keegan. He's Guthrie's wife's first husband—if you can follow that this late."

He sipped his coffee and seemed to fight for a civil response. "That's one of Collinson's aka's—an early one. Let me tell you about Collinson first. To be fair about this you have to have the full picture on him."

"Okay." I drank some laced coffee.

"Nothing to smoke, I suppose—cigar, cigarillo . . . ?"

"Hilde despises smokers. Calls them EC's."

124

"What's that?"

"Emphysema candidates. Get on with it."

"Collinson got into the big-time in the Vietnam War days. He was one of the conduits the Yanks used to ship the heroin out of South-east Asia back to the States."

"How did they get it down here? Why bother?"

"A hundred ways. GI's and Australians on leave brought it in; vehicles coming down to be serviced; the post; parachutes for re-packing was a good way, they tell me. Well, Collinson was a collection point and he passed it on to people who took it Stateside. Then he got into that angle himself. Why? Australia was thought of as squeaky-clean in those days. What did the bloody Yanks know about the place? Kangaroos and tennis players. Nobody looked twice at stuff and people coming in from here. It's different now, after the Mr. Asia thing."

"I bet."

"Collinson was in the big money, very big. He used it to expand—supplied girls to the brass, supplied the drugs where they were needed. Did you know that some of the U.S. boys wouldn't fight unless they had their grass."

I shook my head.

"That's right. Wouldn't fight. Or they'd collaborate to get it."

"Well, some wars are just big arms deals, really."

"Yeah. Collinson had more cash than he knew what to do with, and he set up a loans and finance firm to launder it. He's an accounting genius as well as a crook. One thing led to another; the war ended, and he had these links with organised crime in the States."

I yawned. "Come on!"

"It's true—for money-washing mainly; he bought a bank in the Philippines. All this is in the seventies—not the finest hour for legitimate government, you'll recall. Who could kick? Collinson and blokes like him got away with murder, and millions. But he was smarter than most—didn't make a splash, kept his head down, confused his identity. He used the phone or intermediaries—no one ever saw him, hardly."

"Like Howard Hughes," I said. I'd heard something of this—with other names and deals—from Harry Tickener. It was something I'd always stayed well clear of: it was the world in which the directors of one company were the principals in another which held major stock in company controlled by the one you first thought of.

"I wouldn't know about that," Parker said. "I'm more parochial in my interest. We've got a bloody huge file on him. Now."

"What about then?"

"He had some very solid protection—police, government, possibly Intelligence—who knows? He's still got some of it. His operation got blown by the Marchant Enquiry—did you follow that?"

I nodded. Mr. Justice Marchant's brief had been to investigate Customs Department corruption wherever he might find it. But the thing had got out of hand, and had spilled over into the administration of justice and the workings of the financial system. It was still going on— sputtering into life from time to time—despite high-level efforts to snuff it. A lot of big fish had been caught—and even more had been badly scared.

"Our information was that Collinson got wind of the Enquiry's interest in him, and he started to liquidate. He had a partner . . . hold on, talking's making me dry . . ."

He took a sip of his coffee and I reflected on what a strain it must have been staying abreast of all this changing information. And he'd said he was doing other things as well.

"Barratt," he went on. "CB Holdings Limited—Collinson and Barratt. That's where I came in. Don't know why, but Collinson killed Barratt. Maybe they argued about the

126

wind-up, or maybe Collinson didn't want anyone around who knew as much as Barratt did. There was a suggestion that he sort of threw him out as a decoy, scapegoat; call it what you like. Anyway, he shot him. Barratt was worth peanuts by then. That's a year or so ago; Collinson's thought to be in Australia, in Sydney even. But no one knows where."

"What's 'thought to be' mean?"

"Phone calls get made—they've been recorded. Things still get done."

"Why wouldn't he skip?"

"Don't know. Thinks he's safe? Got a woman? He's sick? Scared of flying? Don't know."

I'd finished the coffee and scotch and was thinking about another. I decided against it. I hadn't even had my say yet. I poured some coffee, straight.

"You seem to know a hell of a lot about him."

"Might sound that way, but I don't know. I've got facts and dates and figures, but I don't feel that I understand him. Don't know what makes him tick." He flexed his fingers. "They put me in charge of a task force." He snorted. "Task force! We didn't come up with anything solid so they disbanded us. Then they disbanded me."

"You're taking it personally, Frank. I don't blame you, but look at it from my angle. Hayes and Catchpole are using young Guthrie as some sort of bait. Let's say they're corrupting him, really screwing him up. All that to get at Collinson, who doesn't mean a dog's fart to me."

Parker drained his cup and gave himself a short whisky. He didn't respond, didn't even blink as I went on.

"I know what you want. You want to let Hayes and Catchpole get on with it. Flush Collinson out—just so long as you're there when he surfaces. You won't care who gets hurt."

"I suppose that's about it."

"I can't let that happen. My job is to unravel the Guthrie kid's problems and straighten him out. Maybe I can do that just with a good heart-to-heart, knowing what I know now."

"I doubt it."

"I've got the Brisbane stuff to work with, remember. Hayes did a job on Ray Guthrie's brother—got him hooked on junk, it looks like. That'll count for something."

"If that kid'll confirm it."

"I think he will."

"You have to consider the hold Dottie Williams might have on him. That could be bloody strong—he's just a kid, Dottie could be his dream woman."

"Yeah."

We faced each other silently across the table; Parker rubbed his bristle, moving his hand tiredly in a clockwise motion.

"We could sleep on it," he said.

"No, we need some ground rules, right now. We're about square—neither of us owes the other a thing. We can get up from here and go about it in our own different ways."

"That couldn't be the smart thing to do."

"Did you push Spotswood off the roof?"

He gaped at me. "No."

"All right, I had to ask."

"Look, Cliff, I'm a bit desperate about this, I know. I am taking it personally. But it hasn't got to me that much. We can't afford to split up. Hayes is good, really good. The fee he'd be on must be enormous. He'll go all the way for it. The whole thing is bound to be messy."

"That's why I should take the Guthrie kid out now."

"Maybe. If you could find him, and if he'd go. Neither sounds real likely to me."

"The kid doesn't know what he's involved in. He doesn't know Collinson's his father. He's in the dark."

"That's tough. But this is bigger than that. Collinson

owns policemen, he own politicians. While that goes on no one's safe, everything's up for grabs."

"It was like that in Jericho, probably, and Athens and Rome. I'm not a crusader."

"It'd be nice to get him." He named one of the government ministers who'd go down with Collinson, and I had to admit that that prospect had a strong appeal. I could feel myself coming around, and Parker knew it.

"I'll try not to hurt the kid if it comes to something rugged. You'd be there, that'd be your job. I wouldn't want to hurt anyone except Hayes and Collinson." He grinned. "Especially not you or me."

"What would the next move be, then?"

"To check on my bloke in Parramatta. Tiny said they were worried about that. I'll worry 'em some more."

"What happened to Tiny could worry them too."

"Right. I feel we could get the initiative, with a bit of luck."

That decided me, plus the feeling that I had one long shot that could give *me* the initiative. I could make my moves about Ray Guthrie when the time came. I looked at Parker's shadowed, weary eyes—if the thoughts behind them were private, so were mine. I put some whisky in my cup and clinked it with Frank's.

"Co-operation," I said.

"Talk some more tomorrow?"

I nodded, he went to the bathroom and then up the stairs. When I heard Hilde's door close I pulled the telephone over.

Helen's voice was sexy, I decided, even at 1:30 A.M.

"It's 1:30," she said.

"Do you want to see me or not?"

"I do."

"Keep your finger near the buzzer."

15

In the morning we did the coffee and toast routine in reverse. It was late when I came into the bedroom, juggling the plates and mugs; the sun slanting in through the window had warmed the room up, and Helen lay naked on her front on top of the bed. I looked at her wide shoulders, marked by the swimsuit straps and the hollows and curves lower down. Her long toes were hooked over the end of the bed and I could see the muscle, like a rounded W in outline, in her calves. She had dancer's legs. She heard the crockery rattle.

"I'd like you to rub oil into every inch of my body," she said.

"Can I drink my coffee first? Which hand do you want me to use?"

"And then I want to go to a beach where we can swim naked. Can you take the time, Cliff?"

I put the mugs and plate down by the bed and began rubbing both hands over her back. Her skin was smooth and her spine felt supple and strong, like a whip.

"One phone call and I'm free."

She half-turned around and reached down for her coffee; it was about the first movement not connected with sex she'd made since my arrival at 2 A.M. She drank the coffee in a couple of gulps, the way I usually do myself. She ate a piece of toast. Then she put her face close to mine and looked at me as if she was counting the crow's feet.

"Something bad happened last night," she said. "You fucked me to help you to forget about it."

"Not exactly."

"Yes, you did. It was terrific; I'm not complaining." She held out her cup. "Now I want some more coffee and some toast and the oil, and I want to hear about it."

Parker sounded grouchy on the phone, as if he and Hilde had struck their first reef. We agreed to meet later in the day to review procedure, but I had a feeling that the Hardy-Parker accord would prove uneasy.

Helen had a red Camira, one of the kind they drove from Sydney to Melbourne on less than a tank of petrol. The way she drove she'd be lucky to make it to Gundagai. She was a fast, aggressive driver with a good traffic sense, and a fine disregard for the workings of the machine.

Lady Bay is at the top of the peninsula, one bay on from Camp Cove. I thought I knew the way but I gave Helen a wrong direction and we ended up within the bounds of the Naval Base Watson. A land-locked sailor, with one of those shaves you can rub with a cigarette paper and not hear a sound and wearing starched, knee-length shorts, steered us right with a leer.

The deal is that you park at Camp Cove, which is a topless but not bottomless beach, and walk around the cliffs a kilometre or so to Lady Bay. Helen was wearing loose, light-blue trousers, a striped tee-shirt and sandals. She climbed the fence, jumped across gaps between the concrete slabs, and negotiated the gun emplacements which were built to repel an invader that never came. Her dark-red, cropped hair shone like polished stone when the sun caught it, and she moved effortlessly, like an expert bushwalker.

I brought up the rear, carrying the bag and the towels and feeling the sweat running down under my shirt. It was hot

131

with no wind; it was too early for the sea breeze, and the still, warm air gave the sea sounds a special clarity—the noise of the birds, the water against the cliffs and the scrape of Helen's sandals on the rocks.

The nude bathing beach looks to have been designed by Nature for the purpose; you reach it by going backwards ten metres down a ladder attached to a sheer drop. The distance was about the same as Tiny Spotswood's fall, but here you descended from grass to sand, by wood not metal, and in the full clean light of the sun. The top of the cliff is a flat sward and there, fully-clothed, with their legs dangling over the edge, sat three men with their eyes fixed on the people below. I went down the ladder after Helen and we stood on the sand and surveyed the sixty metre beach, flanked at both ends by rocks.

All the sun bathers were men; they were very tanned and most were muscular. They lay and sat, very still, and seemed to be thinking about stillness.

"It's a *tableau vivant*," Helen whispered.

"What's that?"

"Look it up."

"You're the only broad on the beach."

"Somehow that seems more novel than taking the clothes off."

We took the clothes off, just dropped them and the bag where we stood, and ran down to the water. It was cool, a bit cloudy and very deep within a few metres of the shore. Helen waded a few steps, dived and went underwater for about ten metres. She surfaced and swam seawards with long, easy strokes. I ploughed along after her with my Maroubra-basic stroke, and we swam well out to where the water was translucent and cold. We trod water and touched each other.

"I was going to say how does a country girl like you get

to swim like that, then I remembered that you're not a country girl."

"Coogee," she said. "Remember the trams?"

We paddled around for a while, and then swam in. Stretched out on the sand, side by side, we joined the statuary. A quarter of an hour of that, and Helen started to giggle.

"I can't take this; it's like being in Madame Tussaud's."

We were back at her place, drinking coffee, when I finally got around to telling her the shape and substance of the Guthrie case. I'd already told her about Spotswood's fall, this was the context. I sanitised it a bit. I told her about Parker.

"He sounds ruthless."

"He's not generally, or I used not to think so. This seems to have made him harder. People don't realise what being a cop is like, especially a Homicide detective. It's not all free beers and fucks. In a funny way, a cop is what he does. An honest, energetic cop like Parker is very honest; uncomfortably so, maybe."

"What about you? Do you become what you do?"

I smiled. "Not as much. That's one of the reasons I'm not a cop. Tell me about Michael."

"Mike. No one calls him Michael."

"I felt Mike was a bit informal, under the circumstances."

"What *are* the circumstances, Cliff?"

"God knows. How much of your first six months have you really got left?"

"Hours."

"Let's not waste 'em."

We went back to bed with enthusiasm and success. There was a good deal of tenderness too, for the first time. I learned a bit more about Mike; that he farmed everything

133

from pigs to grapes; that he operated a small cannery; that he worked twenty hours a day.

"He's in love with the land," she said.

"Uh huh."

"He's writing a book about it."

"When? In his sleep?"

I only got information about her by way of trade. She'd been a librarian in Sydney before meeting and marrying Michael Broadway, teacher turned gentleman farmer. She'd done a degree by correspondence, and got first class honours in English.

"I'm depressed," I said.

"Why?"

"I dropped out after one year of Law. I passed Constitutional History and Criminal Law—failed Contracts and Torts."

"What're Torts?"

"I forget."

Helen's advice on my professional problem was to get hold of Ray Guthrie, tell him everything I knew, and detach him from the criminal element.

"He might be part of the criminal element himself by now," I said. "And there's his attitude to his real father to consider. I just don't know how powerful a feeling that is. You're a parent, tell me about what children feel for their parents."

"Parents don't know what they feel."

"There you are, then."

"It sounds as if it'll all end in grief," she said. "I'm sorry, but that's how it sounds to me."

"That's why I have to stick with it and see it through in something like Parker's terms. Not exactly his, but to some sort of resolution. If I'm on the spot, maybe I can cut down on the grief a bit."

"I hope so."

134

* * *

My arrangement with Parker was to meet him back at my place at around seven. That gave me several hours for my long shot. Mahoney Place is a narrow, one-way street in Surry Hills which runs off South Dowling Street, opposite Moore Park. I left my car in a lane nearby and walked in the park for a while, watching some kids risking their lives at grass skiing. I was trying to change gear out of "tenderness" and into "work." Kids having a good time on the grass didn't quite do it—maybe if one of them had broken his neck.

Right now, "work" meant going to make enquiries about a private detective named Phillips; "loathsome" in at least one person's memory, who had pursued our noble calling in Mahoney Place twenty years before. It was hard to do without at least one decent drink inside me.

The street was narrow enough for a ball thrown against a brick fence on one side to rebound and hit the opposite fence on the full. That's if you were good enough to judge the force and distance right; the kids who were playing this game halfway down the street were good enough. There were two of them—Mediterraneans—taking it in turns. I grinned at them and they stopped to let me pass—the coordination and the sweat on their faces was reassuring in the pinball age.

Number 32 was a white-painted brick wall, built on the street line with a door in it, no window. TOTAL GRAPHICS was painted in red on the bricks in metre-high letters. I knocked, reflecting that maybe I'd be more successful if I called myself TOTAL INVESTIGATIONS.

The man who opened the door looked pretty successful in his field, if clothes maketh the man: he wore a velvet shirt open to the waist, revealing a bushel of hair and a kilo of gold charms and medallions. His legs were stick-thin inside

135

tight leather pants. His head was shaved and he wore a diamond stud in one ear. The shaved head gave him that exhibitionist look it always does. Otherwise, he was normal. He went back inside as soon as he'd pulled the door open and I had no choice but to follow him.

It was a long time back since it had been a private detective's office. That would be just a bad memory. Now the deep, narrow room was scrupulously clean. Light came in through a bank of skylights high up on one wall. A long bench held half a dozen VDT screens, each with a chair in front of it. There was a large bank of Swedish-looking storage baskets filled with paper and a bookcase half-filled with books whose spines looked all the same. A desk as big as a pool table was covered with coffee-making gear—an urn, filter machine, a grinder, packets of coffee, and filter papers.

Baldy practically ran back along the bench and threw himself down in front of one of the screens.

"Be with you in a minute," he said. "This is nearly out. Bloody exciting."

Nice to see a man happy in his work, I thought. I closed the door behind me and walked in. "Graphics" suggested paper and pens to me, scissors and set squares. Apart from the paper in the bins there was nothing like that. A big photocopier was in the corner, and here at least there was some frivolous paper—a big poster of Orson Welles as Charles Foster Kane—I was surprised it wasn't a holograph.

The bald man's hands danced over the keys and he tapped his sneakered foot as if he was playing Scott Joplin. I looked over his shoulder but couldn't make anything of the zig-zag flashes that appeared on the screen.

"Got it!" he bawled. "Fucking A!" He swivelled around and stood up. Two long strides took him to the coffee table, and his leather pants didn't split.

136

"Coffee?"

"Okay. Thanks."

He shovelled coffee into a filter paper, fitted it into the machine and poured the water from a plastic jug. The machine was already hot, and the water hit the element with a loud hiss.

"Boil the water first. That's the secret."

I nodded. "I boil the water and then pour it in on top of the powder."

He shrugged, stagily. "Barbarian. Well, what can I do for you?"

He took two polystyrene cups from a metre-high stack and set them on the table. He put two spoons of raw sugar into one and looked enquiringly at me. I nodded and held up one finger—I thought I might need the energy to keep up with him. He jigged while the coffee dripped through. When the beaker was half-full with liquid the colour of shellac, he poured.

"Here you go. I live on the stuff—it calms me down."

I drank; the coffee was strong enough to clean drains.

"I'm trying to locate a man named Phillips." I put the cup down, dug out one of my cards and handed it over. "He was in the same business as me, and he had an office at this address. Some time back."

He looked at the card and shook his head. *Dead-end,* I thought. "You don't know him, that right?"

He fiddled with the stud in his ear. "I didn't say that."

"You shook your head."

"I was shaking my head at the terrible design of this card." He flicked it with his forefinger's long nail. "Look at that lettering. *De*-pressing! That's no way to win business, Mr. Hardy."

"I'll get a new one designed," I said. "I might give you the job if you can help me."

He did some more stud twiddling. "Have a look at this." He rummaged in a drawer and came up with a pile of cards held together with an elastic band. He flipped one over to me like a croupier. The words TOTAL GRAPHICS stood out black and bold against the gold background.

"Very nice, Mr. . . ?"

"Style—Ian Style, good name isn't it? It's my real one, too." He finished his coffee and poured another; I was still waiting for my tongue to stop throbbing. "You're right, one Phillips had this place before me. That's oh . . . seven years back. You should have seen it. A real mess."

"No style, eh?"

He looked at me. "Oh, God," he groaned. "I think I stopped counting remarks like that at about five thousand."

"I'm sorry."

"It's all right. Yes, Phillips. I kept getting mail for him for years. The re-direction system has never been very effective."

"Where did you send it? Do you have an address for him, did you write it down?"

If he had had any eyebrows they would have shot up, but his head was quite hairless. "Write it down! No chance. We're computerised here—totally."

I smiled, although I didn't think his joke was so much better than mine.

"I've got it on file."

"I'd be grateful if you'd give it to me. I need to see him, urgently."

"Do I get the re-designing job?"

"Sure."

He got up and bounced across to one of the consoles. His fingers got busy, and symbols began scrolling on to the screen. I sneaked a look at the bookshelf—all computer manuals. He punched a key and froze the image.

138

"Here it is. Joshua Phillips, 33A MacDonald Street, Erskineville."

I went back to the nineteenth century, and wrote it down. "When was the last time you got mail for him?"

The screen came alive again and froze.

"About this time last year. An envelope, private. Nothing ever came back. Does that mean the address still applies?"

"I hope so. That's amazingly efficient; I should get a system like that."

"You'll be out of business in five years if you don't. More coffee?"

I refused the coffee, thanked him for the help and he said he'd submit some designs for the card. I thanked him again and let myself out. By that time he was sitting down at a keyboard again and the sneakers were beating a tattoo.

Erskineville has been hit by the middle class money only in patches. Most of it retains the old atmosphere of toil— awkwardly angled streets built for foot and horse traffic, and a mix of residential and factory buildings. A few of the terrace houses are wide and rise to three storys, but most are more modest and some get down to the narrowness of 33A MacDonald Street. The house was so narrow that my car, parked exactly outside, seemed to overlap its boundaries.

The tiny place crouched behind a privet hedge three or four metres back from the street; that put its front door about forty metres from the railway line. A train rattled past as I pulled open the rickety gate. The line was on a viaduct over the road, and with the wind in the right quarter it must have sounded in 33A as if the trains were coming through the front window.

It was 4:30 in the afternoon, a time when there were a lot of reasons to be out. It occurred to me that I should have asked Style for Phillips's phone number which he would surely have had on file, along with his blood type and date of birth.

The man in striped pyjamas who answered the door to my knock looked as if he'd have a blood type all his own. His skin was white as few skins are; his sparse hair was white as were his eyebrows—his fiercely bloodshot eyes were all the more alarming in the almost colourless face. It was impossible to guess his age—I was having trouble with his species. He was a whole head shorter than me, so I got the red eyes upturned—an unnerving sight.

"Have you brought it?" he said.

"Brought what?"

"I rang up the bottle shop; they said they'd send it round if they had time." The red eyes looked at me and judged me not to be a delivery person. "I guess they didn't have time."

"Are you Joshua Phillips? Used to have an office in Mahoney Place?"

"Yes. Phillips. That's me." His voice was reedy, as if it was wearing out. "Who're you?"

I gave him one of my despised cards. He pulled spectacles out of his pyjama jacket pocket and looked at the card.

"It's a mug's game."

"Maybe. I'm after information on a case you handled nearly twenty years ago. How's your memory?"

The red glare dimmed and his eyes went cunning.

"It improves with money and sweet sherry."

"Okay." I stepped back. "What brand?"

He grinned, showing two teeth, maybe three. There were thickets of white hair in his ears and in his nostrils. He cackled at me. "Flagon brand."

The pub was ten minutes away by foot. I came back with a flagon of sherry for him and two cans of light beer for me.

He let me in and we went down a dark, narrow passage to a kitchen which was lit by a single, naked bulb. The broken part of the window was blanked out with masonite; the unbroken part was so dirty that no light could penetrate. He put the flagon on a shaky, laminex-topped table which stood on an uneven floor covered with cracked, lifting linoleum.

He shuffled around in the tiny room until he found what he was looking for—a sherry glass with a gold band around it and a creamy residue in the bottom. There was a strong, mouldy smell of neglect, and I couldn't tell whether it came from the room or the man, or both. I accepted Phillips's offer of a chair at the table, ripped open one of the cans and put its clean edge to my mouth. He got the top off the flagon by sawing through the perforations with a blunt knife. He filled his glass, spilling a little on the table.

"Cheers," he said.

"Cheers. Let's have a talk, Mr. Phillips."

"Let's see the money."

I got twenty dollars out of my wallet, and put the note under the flagon.

"I can take the sherry and the money away with me if I want."

He nodded, and tossed down the drink in one gulp. "I couldn't stop you. I'm arthritic, don't get around too good any more." He looked as if he'd never got around too good; his small, bent body had a frailness, a hospitalised look. He wouldn't have been the man you hired when you wanted some muscle work done. If he'd made a living he must have had brains. He poured himself another brimming glass, drank half of it and topped it up.

"Do you remember a case you handled nearly twenty years ago? To do with a man named Keegan—Peter Keegan?"

He looked at me, blankly.

"You were hired by the estranged wife. Her name was Pat, maybe she was using the married name, maybe not. A small, dark, very good-looking woman. Two kids. She wanted the dope on the man she'd married; he'd turned out different from what she'd thought. Anything clicking?"

He held up his glass and looked at the golden liquid inside the dirty vessel as if it was the most beautiful thing in the world. "Mrs. Patricia Keegan," he said dreamily. "Athletic figure. Good mind. Low on money, high on pride. The husband was a wrong'un—sly grog, betting, whores, you name it."

"You remember all this?"

"I wrote reports; I read 'em over. They're my favourite reading." He drank and poured again, both rapidly.

I got my photograph of the man in uniform and showed it to him. He got the spectacles out of the pyjama pocket again, wiped them on a sleeve which smeared them, and looked closely at the photo.

"That's him. Younger, of course. Put on a bit 'a weight by the time I was on the job."

"How did you go about it?"

He probed with a corner of my card inside a filthy fingernail, pried out the dirt and flicked it on the floor. "You should know—ask around, stay up late, get up early, surveillance and observation."

"Where did Keegan live at that time?" I tried to keep the question neutral, but he detected the increased interest. He sipped his drink and didn't reply. I drank some beer and tried to wait him out, but he held the cards and he knew it.

"How much?"

"Fifty," he said.

"It's a long time ago, the chances . . ."

"Are bloody good that he's where I say he is. He lived in

Mosman, but he had another place—a special sort of place."

I took out two twenties and a ten, and put them under the flagon. He'd poured carelessly; sherry had run down the side and now Henry Lawson's head was bisected by a dark, sticky ring. Henry wouldn't have minded.

"Place called Hacking Inlet, d'you know it?"

I shook my head.

"Little place in the National Park. They let people put houses up around there until just after the war. Then they stopped it. Place can't ever get any bigger. This Keegan had a fibro shack down there—little dump, end of a dead-end lane, steep hill behind it, and the bloody water on his doorstep. Nothing to look at from the outside, but I got a chance to have a close gander and a bit of a look inside. Very different bill of goods: big garage underneath. Looked from the lane like there was no driveway down to it, but there was. Bloody warehouse that garage—tinned food, fuel, booze, the lot. Withstand a siege. All mod cons— heating, flash plumbing. All inside this little dump you wouldn't look at twice."

"Quiet place is it?"

"Real quiet, except for the summer season when it'd fill up, I suppose. Be busy now, but there's limits on what it can hold, see. Limits on the dunnies, 'cos of the land and the septic tanks and that. An' you know what those places are like. Everyone turns off their brains when they get to the weekender or the holiday place. Bloody great hide-out."

I finished my can of beer and set it down carefully on the scarred table. This sounded like the real thing. A man in Collinson's game needed a bolthole, and this Hacking Inlet couldn't be that far from the GPO.

"Did he have many visitors?"

143

He shook his head. "Zero. I followed him there twice. Stayed a coupla' days—no women, no men, just him."

"How did he strike you?"

"Bloody dangerous."

"Did you tell the wife about this place?"

He'd had another sherry while I was doing my thinking; the level was down past the top of the label and the red glow in his eyes was like a three-unit fire. He nodded, but he was losing control and his head was loose on his scrawny neck like a puppet's.

"Honest operation. Put everything in the report. Honest as the day's long. That's why I'm here, like this."

"Who else would know about this—the surveillance and the place at Hacking Inlet?"

His red eyes went shrewd again and he poured another glass; I jerked it away from him and spilled half on the table.

"Anyone else?"

"Had a partner," he mumbled. "Diddled me, a' course, useless bastard."

"You had a partner when you did the Keegan job?"

"Had 'im twenty years."

I was amused, despite myself. "Twenty years? A useless bastard?"

"Well, he was a useful bastard, too. Yeah, Wally Bigelow, junior partner."

"How much would he know about the Keegan case?"

"I've got no show of rememberin' unless you let me have another drink."

I nodded and he recovered the glass and filled it; he had to use both hands to support the flagon and its neck and the top of the glass rattled like maracas. He transferred the two hands to the glass and got it up to his mouth where he held it, sipping. When he had drunk half of it I reached out and took the glass. I put it down on the table in front of him. He cupped his shaking hands around it.

"Wally only knew about it in outline. He'd know the name, and he knew what sort of bloke this Keegan was. He didn't do any of the work though, I did it all."

"Would he have known about the hide-out?"

"No."

"Where is he now?"

His look was half-mournful, half-triumphant. "He's dead. The business went to pot, Wally wasn't any help. Bigger drunk 'n me at the end. I found out he was sellin' the stuff to the other side. Y' know—wives an' husbands and that. We split up. Sort of stayed in touch for a while; we were mates, really. Then he went to Queensland for his health. Then I heard he was dead."

"When?"

"Oh, just recent, last coupla' months."

He lifted the glass and drank the rest of the sherry. I looked down at the money on the table and tried to calculate how many flagons it would buy him. Not enough. There weren't enough. I stood up and he pushed the other can of beer across the table.

"Never touch that stuff," he said, "doesn't do you any good."

16

They were waiting for me when I got home, and I have to admit they did it well. I pushed open the front door with the details of my interview with Phillips still being sorted in my head, half-expecting Parker and Hilde to be screwing on the stairs, and "Bully" Hayes stepped out of the door immediately to the right of the front door. He slapped the side of my head with a heavy hand made heavier by the automatic pistol in it.

"That's for Tiny, Hardy," he said. "And just an instalment."

My gun was in the car, and my wits were loose with surprise.

"Nothing to say?" His Queensland drawl was more suggestive of Boggo Road Gaol than Great Keppel Island.

"I'll listen, I think."

"That'd be smart for openers."

Liam Catchpole and Dottie Williams came out of the front room into the hallway. Liam was still so slimy-looking you hoped he wouldn't touch the walls. Dottie had got fatter; her thighs under her mini skirt were meaty, and her double chin creased as she bent her head to light a cigarette. She dropped the match on the sea grass matting.

"You'll start a fire, Dottie," I said.

Hayes hit me again, same place, same way. "Manners," he said. "Let's go and sit down."

I had my ears cocked for the familiar sounds of my house;

Hilde's radio, the shower she usually left dripping; the window in my room that rattles. Everything sounded reassuringly normal; there was no blood on the sea grass, no whiff of cordite in the air. I hoped Frank and Hilde were away somewhere, eating Italian.

We went to the back of the house, and Catchpole and Williams sat down at the table. They were quiet, as if they were depressed. Hayes backed me up against the sink and stood close, threateningly. He was a little taller than me and much broader. He was well groomed; shaved close and recently barbered; his business shirt looked expensive and had kept its creases that late in the day; his tie was carefully knotted, exactly centred. The downturned mouth made him look as if he'd never been happy.

Catchpole picked up a knife and fiddled with it, excavating the grooves in the pine table. "You killed Tiny," he said.

"He fell. Accident."

"You took him away," Catchpole said; he dug the knife in an inch and twisted. "You picked him up at the Crimea, you and some other cunt. You took him away in that fuckin' bomb you drive."

I didn't say anything, on the principle that fear will find words to express itself. I was full of it. Catchpole levered up a long splinter from the table top, and worked at it.

"To save time," Hayes said, "I'm going to assume that you know who I am. That gutless wonder of a Tiny would've told you that."

I nodded.

"Good. Now, you've been working for Guthrie, and getting right in my way."

Silence looks like fear, too, I thought. You can't win. I shrugged. "Had to protect the boy. Trying to."

"You haven't done much of a job. Know where he is now?"

I shook my head.

"Neither do I. All I know is he's no fucking good to me anymore. I'm under pressure all of a sudden. I don't like that. I like to apply the pressure myself."

"We all do."

"Don't be smart. We don't think you're smart. Liam and Dottie here want me to put you away for killing Tiny. They're not smart, either."

"No quarrel with me there."

"You're doing it again. Must've got you into a lot of trouble, that."

Catchpole had worked the sliver of wood out and was digging in another spot. Williams smoked and patted her soft chin.

"*I* am smart," Hayes said. "I have to be. I've got a contract to kill Peter Collinson, and I want to collect on it. I don't care about Spotswood, I don't care about the Guthrie kid."

I turned around, ran the water and washed my hands in the sink. Hayes looked surprised, but he let me do it. I flicked at the paper towel holder and pulled off enough to dry my hands. There were beads of sweat above the wrinkles on Hayes's forehead, where his hairline would once have been. It was the only sign that he was in any way affected by the exterior world.

"Why were you working on the Guthrie kids? What was the idea?"

"Collinson kept his eye on his kids, right up to when the shit hit the fan. He worried about them. I'm one of the few people who knew that. Nobody else knew he even had any kids. I reckoned that by screwing up the kids I could get him

148

to show himself, or give me a lead. I'm good at it—I wouldn't need much, believe me."

"Didn't work," I said.

"It would've. I had the time and the people I needed. Had those Guthrie kids watched round the clock. Now the game's all changed. You're sniffing around, and the word is your mate Parker could be getting close to Collinson his way. I thought I could cancel him out, but it looks like he's tougher than that. I want to know what he knows and what you know, Hardy. I don't want to miss my chance at Collinson. There's too much money at stake."

"You have my sympathy."

"Do you ever say anything that isn't smart-arsed?"

"I mean it." My mind had been roaring around the problem, looking for a way to handle it, and now I thought I'd found it. Selling anything to Hayes, though, would be a hard sell.

"Look, Collinson's nothing to me. I found out that he's still married to the kid's mother. No divorce. Paul Guthrie's a jealous man. Collinson dead would suit him just fine."

"What's he yapping about?" Williams snapped.

"Shut up, Dottie," Hayes said. "Go on, Hardy. What about Parker?"

"All Parker wants is his job back. He's not interested in being a hero. Just let me nut this out . . . If Collinson's dead, the people who put the screws on Parker because he might just have got Collinson alive and talking, well, they can relax and go to bed. They'd be the ones who hired you."

Hayes nodded. "I suppose so. I don't give a fuck. I've got guarantees and safeguards, that's all I care about."

"If Parker can pick up a few crumbs from this, he'd be sweet. He's an honest cop, but he's not a crusader."

"Honest cop," Catchpole sneered, and did some more

knife work. The scotch bottle was still on the table. I took two steps across the room, picked it up and slammed it down on Catchpole's fingers. He yelped, and the knife skittered away.

"Shit in your own nest, Catchpole."

He jumped up and faced me, but there was no fight in him, really. His eyes darted around, and I realised what he was doing—looking for Tiny. Hayes moved across and took the bottle from my hand. Catchpole subsided, and Dottie Williams lit her sixth or seventh cigarette. Hayes got a glass from the sink and poured himself a measure of scotch and tossed it down. The phone rang; Williams, who was sitting nearest to it, jumped. The phone kept ringing.

I looked at it; we all looked at it. Hayes nodded at me to answer it and gestured at Catchpole to get out of the way. Hayes stuck his ear down close to hear—whatever move he made, the automatic was never vulnerable to attack, and he let nothing get between it and me.

"Mr. Hardy?"

"Yes. Who's this?"

"It's Jess Polansky, Mr. Hardy. Ray Guthrie's girl-friend?"

"Yes, Jess. What's up?"

"It's Ray. He's just gone. I'm scared. He's crazy . . . wild . . ."

"You're all right? Not hurt?"

"No."

"Okay, calm down. Tell me what happened."

Hayes snapped his fingers at Williams; she poured him another drink and passed it across. I could have done with one myself.

"He came up to Newport. He just dragged me out of the office, pulling me and shouting. He said Chris was dead. He called his father . . . everything . . . every word. Said he was going to kill him." She paused. "He wrecked the Guthries' boat."

"What boat?"

"They've got a sort of houseboat up here, almost that. He went down into the living quarters and ripped everything up. He was shouting and swearing."

"What? Shouting what?"

"I don't know. He kept saying there must be something. He was looking for something."

"Did he find it?"

"He found something in with his mother's things. Some papers. He just left the mess, and me. He just left." Sobbing, deep and convulsive, came over the wire.

"Jess! Jess! Listen! Do you know where he was going? Did he say?"

"No. No. I don't know what to do. I don't know where Mr. Guthrie is . . ."

I clamped my hand over the receiver and looked at Hayes. "I think I know where he's going. I think I know where Collinson is. I know what the kid found. Can we do a deal?"

"Collinson's mine."

I nodded. "The kid's out of it?"

"All right. Get rid of her!"

I gave Helen Broadway's number to Jess, and told her to keep calling it until she got through. Helen would help her, I said. Jess calmed down, repeated the number a couple of times which seemed to soothe her and said she'd do it.

I hung up, got up from the table and poured myself a drink.

"What the fuck was all that about?" Dottie put her foot on another butt on the floor.

"Hardy's going to take us to Collinson. Wouldn't care to

give us the address, Hardy?" Hayes took a length of paper towel and blotted those sweat beads.

I shook my head. "I want to see to the kid. I want to see Collinson dead, if that's the way it has to be."

"I don't trust the cunt," Catchpole said.

"Don't be bloody stupid!" Hayes wadded the paper towel and threw it at the open tidy bin. He missed. "We're not talking about trust here, we're talking business. Still, you'll have to give me a bit more, Hardy. Convince me you know where Collinson is."

It was the right question for him to ask.

"I know where you got the information about Collinson's kids," I said. "From a guy named Wally Bigelow, used to be a private detective."

"That's right," Hayes said.

"What happened to Wally?"

"He dropped dead. I was about to put some pressure on him to give out a bit more. He sold me some of it, but not enough. Bloody old pisspot. Died of fright."

"He didn't know any more. Twenty years ago he was partners with a private detective named Phillips. Collinson's wife hired Phillips to check on her husband. Collinson went by another name then. He'd begun to organise himself, be Mr. Anonymous, but he wasn't quite there. I've talked to Phillips."

"So we could talk to Phillips," Williams said.

"No," I lied. "I've tucked him away. You can't get to him."

"What'd this Phillips have to say?" Hayes was calm, weighing his words.

"He reckoned Collinson had a place to hide in. A perfect place, it sounds."

"When was this?" Catchpole said.

"Nearly twenty years ago."

152

"Shit! Twenty years! Everything's different!"

"I wouldn't say that. You're just as slimy as you were then."

"Knock it off," Hayes snarled. "It *is* a long time, Hardy." He looked dubious, and convincing him was the key to the whole thing. I had one more card to play. "I've got what seems to be the only known photograph of Collinson," I said. "Put that bloody gun away, look reasonable, and I'll let you see it. The Guthrie kid in Brisbane's going to be all right. I got him to the hospital, so I'm in good there. If I walk away with the other one, I'm on a bonus. I want a deal as much as you, Hayes."

The idea of the photograph excited him—police training maybe—and the money talk was a clincher. He understood that sort of motive. Dealing with him was like trying to walk on a slippery, sloping roof, but I had as much duplicity as he did, and neither of us had handholds. He put the automatic on the table.

"We're dealing. Let's see the picture."

I got out the old photograph and passed it to him. He examined it like a violinist with a Stradivarius.

"Well, I'm buggered."

Dottie Williams leaned over and looked. "Looks like the picture the kid talked about. Said he had it, then he couldn't come up with it. Said it'd been pinched."

"How'd you get to him, Hayes? The kid, how'd you get to him?"

Hayes grinned. "Dottie got to him."

"He was as green as grass," she said. "The first hand job I gave him blew his mind." On closer inspection the pale-red aureole of her hair was a dyed, teased fake; her clothes reeked of tobacco, kissing her would be like licking an ashtray. But maybe I was getting discriminating as I got older. Liam Catchpole broke in with a typical contribution.

153

"Who needs Hardy?" he said. "Let's get what he knows out of him and go and do the job. Fuck Hardy! Fuck the kid."

Hayes seemed to give the idea some consideration, then he shook his head. "We haven't got the time. Ray's on the move, and Christ knows what'll happen if he gets to Collinson first. If he's as crazy as his bird says he is, he could kill him, or they could take off for Aca-fucking-pulco or somewhere. Besides," he looked at Catchpole, who was propped back against the sink where I'd been, "you reckon you can put the scarers on Hardy?"

A lot of the stuffing had gone out of Catchpole since I'd last seen him. His reputation was more for slipperiness than gutsiness, but neither was apparent now. His face was tense and pale, acne-pitted, and he was pushing back his lank, oiled hair with nervous flicks. There was a brown scuff mark across the toe of his right, white shoe.

"I could if I had Tiny here," he muttered.

"Forget it," Hayes said. That should have been good news for me, but the trouble was it sounded as if he was saying forget Williams, forget Catchpole, forget Guthrie, forget Hardy. Forget everything except Hayes and Collinson. His obsession was strong, maybe stronger than his ability. I had to hope for that, hope for a chance or half a chance.

Hayes finished his drink and put the photograph in his pocket, where it made a dark blur behind the crisp, faint-lined material. "Where are we going, Hardy?"

"South. Thirty miles or so."

"Cautious, eh?"

"That's right, eh."

"You're being a smart-arse again, and I was trying to like you."

"Don't bother. Do we have to take them?"

154

Hayes retrieved his gun and put it away in a holster he wore at the back and on the left-hand side. He was right-handed, and slid the automatic back and away smoothly.

"Yes," he said. "Dottie, would you go and get my jacket from the front room?"

She went out, and Catchpole fidgeted by the sink, very unhappy with it. I consulted the New South Wales road map I keep near the phone books and postcode list.

"Where's Parker?" he snapped.

"He's off with the bird who lives here, probably up her by now." *Forgive me, my friends,* I thought.

Williams came back with the jacket, and Hayes shrugged into it. He adjusted his cuffs and the set of his tie that didn't need attention.

"Want to guess at my fee for this job, Hardy?"

I shook my head.

" 'Course there's expenses, Liam and Dottie are in for a cut. But the fee's half a million dollars. Sort of motivates a man."

"It would," I said.

"Right. Now, I'll go with Hardy, and you two can follow us." He lifted his chin, drawing the loose flesh under there tighter. "Go ahead, Hardy. Make me rich."

17

Hayes pushed the magazines and other junk in the back seat of the Falcon aside, and settled himself there. I tried to comfort myself with the thought that I had a .38 Smith & Wesson Chief's Special an arm's reach away under the dashboard, but no comfort came. Guns are confusing things; I was no match for Hayes with a gun, I knew that, and in a way I was a better match for him without one. That's highly theoretical, and the theory wasn't any comfort either.

Hayes positioned himself directly behind me. "Any way of locking the driver's door?" he said.

"No." I showed him how it opened however the door lock was set.

"Great," he said. "Try that and I'll blow your brains out."

I was about to start the engine, but I held off and half-turned to almost face him. "Would you? Where would that get you? You'd still be in the dark about where Collinson is. It seems to me you need me."

"You're half right, Hardy, but that isn't right enough. I need you for a quick result, that's true. But I can get a result other ways—I could get Mrs. Guthrie to tell me about the private detective she used, and set about finding him. There's the bloke in Parramatta your cop friend Parker is working on. I might do some good with him. Ray Guthrie might be worth twisting. All slower, but Collinson's not leaving the country while he's all hung up about his flesh and blood. I'd get to him sooner or later."

"You said you were under pressure."

"Impatient people," Hayes said moodily. "Let's go."

I turned around and started the motor. "I still don't see why Collinson isn't in Rio."

Hayes cleared his throat; it's true that my car is a bit vulnerable to engine fumes. "Collinson's not finished yet. He's still trying to hang on and save his skin. He must have some supporters still. On the other hand, he's worth half a million dollars to some others."

"Impatient ones."

"Yeah."

"Are you sure you'll get the money?"

"I'll get it."

The roads were clear going south; we went over Tom Ugly's bridge and I had to watch not to be taken off to the coast too early. Everything south of Rockdale is foreign territory to me. A pair of headlights sat squarely and unwaveringly behind me all the way. I played around with the idea of a wild goose chase on which I could lose Catchpole and Williams, and provoke Hayes into some kind of mistake. There were two things against it: I didn't think Hayes would make any mistakes and my job was to protect Ray Guthrie. I was going where I had to go anyway. That Ray was going looking for a man who was worth a half million dead, and that I had the gun that might do the job pointing at the back of my head was just bad luck. *Deep stuff, Hardy.*

As I drove, I thought about Helen Broadway and how she'd react to the call from Jess Polansky. If she was going to have anything to do with me she'd have to get used to such things. Was she going to have anything to do with me? Hi, Mike. How ya doing? I switched to thoughts of Parker and Hilde. Would Parker have displayed my calm, calculated resolve? No. But then, people might be dead who weren't dead yet, including me. Thinking was getting me nowhere. If I wasn't careful, I'd be having regrets.

It was a very uncomfortable drive: the big man sitting behind me didn't fidget, didn't talk; I couldn't hear him breathing. I must have slowed down unconsciously, trying to gain time, hoping for a miracle. He might have fallen asleep.

"Step on it, Hardy. This bomb'll do a bit more than that."

The traffic thinned further along, and the road widened— there was no excuse not to pick up speed. We started to reach dark, ill-lit stretches and curvy sections where a sharp braking might shoot him forward . . . He seemed to read my mind.

"Undo your seat belt, Hardy." He jerked at the fastening above my shoulder. "Any fancy stuff, and you'll go first."

I undid the belt. "I thought we were sort of in this together now. Our interests are pretty much the same."

"Bullshit. My interests have never been the same as anyone else's." He gave a short, unpleasant laugh. "Ask my wife."

It was his only venture into humour, and there was nothing warming about it. I drove, trying to interpret his remark. Was he satisfied or dissatisfied with that state of things? It occurred to me that he might be something of a psychologist—here he had me interpreting his cryptic remarks rather than thinking about my own survival.

I ignored a few signs to Sutherland and Cronulla, hugged the middle lane and thought some more about the .38 and its five cartridges and two inch barrel. A close range gun. I tried to stop thinking about it, in case he really could read my mind. He stirred in his seat.

"Lose them!" he rasped.

"What?"

"Lose that rubbish behind us."

"Jesus, why?"

"They're both useless. Lose them!"

I was getting down to the National Park turnoff and trying to remember its configurations from the one time I'd made the drive. I remembered it as an abrupt swing-off, not well lit.

"Who'll be driving?"

"Liam."

"He any good?"

"Ratshit!"

The lights of Catchpole and Williams's car were a good way back and I could see the trickle of traffic coming up behind them. I accelerated, doused my lights and swung into the left lane, fifty metres before the turn-off. The driver behind me became momentarily confused; I saw his lights waver and then he kept his course. I couldn't look in the rear vision mirror anymore, because I had to concentrate on holding the road at speed with no lights. I took more road than I should and prayed for no on-coming traffic.

I shot down the turn-off and passed the rangers' booth in the middle of the road that marks the entrance to the park. Then the road started to wind and I turned on the lights. I wanted to look back, although the rear vision mirror was blank. Hayes let me feel the gun in the nape of my neck.

"They're gone," he said. "Well done, driver."

18

It's hard to have a meaningful relationship with a man in the back of your car who's holding a gun on you. He'd neatly disposed of some of the distractions—in the persons of Catchpole and Williams—I'd been half-counting on, and he seemed full of purpose and resolution. Unlike me. I asked him about the pair who'd chased me in Elizabeth Bay and his reply was an uninterested grunt.

"Why'd you quit the force, Hayes?" I asked. "You were sitting pretty, weren't you?"

"This came up. One of the conditions was that I left the force. They saw me right, don't worry."

"What will you do with the money?"

Mention of money seemed to relax him a bit; he permitted himself the luxury of a scratch.

"In Queensland you can turn a half million into a whole million pretty fast. And go on from there. If you know the right people. I do."

"Then what?"

"Then the good life, and plenty of it. I'm fifty-four, plenty left in me yet."

"Your turn'll come."

He gave that abbreviated laugh again. "You're a funny bloke, Hardy. You remind me of blokes I knew in the army—shit scared half the time, but they'd still have a go."

There was nothing much to say to that; all I could think to

do was keep the questions up to him, not be passive, and try to act before he decided I was expendable.

"You weren't scared, Hayes? In the service?"

"No."

"Did you know Collinson was in Vietnam?"

"Yeah, I knew. So was I. Never ran across him that I know of."

"What rank did you hold?"

"Warrant Officer. You?"

"Sergeant, briefly."

Lights were coming up behind us fast; Hayes was aware of them as soon as I was.

"Could be them," I said.

"I doubt it. Liam thinks the world ends at Leichhardt—he'd be bushed out here."

"What about Dottie?"

"Dottie only knows one thing. Let them pass and we'll have a look at them."

I slowed and let the car pass; it was a nippy Japanese coupe, carrying two young women. The passenger had her arm around the driver's shoulders. The driver lifted her hand to acknowledge my courtesy and I waved back.

"Dykes," Hayes said.

"None of that in Queensland, eh?"

He didn't do it at once, he waited until a flat, straight stretch and then he clipped me on the ear with the automatic. I felt the flesh tear, and I swerved.

"No more jokes. Just drive."

I drove. I put my hand up and felt the blood on the side of my face. When my ears stopped ringing and the pain had settled to a dull throb, I realised that the blow had had an odd effect on me—I wasn't afraid any more.

The night was clear with a high half-moon; the park stretched away for kilometres on either side of the road. A lot of the growth was small, coming back after the big bushfires of a few years ago. I had the window half-down and was picking up bush smells strongly and, faintly, the smell of the sea.

The sea smell got stronger after we made the first of the turns that would take us to Hacking Inlet. Fifty metres around the turn, Hayes told me to stop. I hit the brakes and pulled on to the gravel. He looked back at the main road and waited. After a minute or so, a car sped past the turn and headed through the park toward the south coast.

"Just making sure," he said. "Let's go."

The road ran flat and straight for a few kilometres, then there was another left turn and a winding descent to Hacking Inlet. The surface was rutted, and I had to grip the wheel hard on some of the turns. We bounced and I wondered if the Chief's Special would fall out. It never had before. I wanted a drink very badly.

The weekenders and holiday houses trickled out along the road from the main settlement, but Phillips was right, the place had none of the signs of being cut up into fish finger blocks the way most of the coastal towns are. Here the trees predominated in wide, deep, seclusion-giving belts between the houses. It was very quiet, and I imagined I could hear the beat of the sea against the sand over the car noise. I drove down until I reached the centre of the township—a general store-cum-petrol-station-cum-pub—a couple of hundred metres back from the beach. It was set in a clearing with a playground and picnic benches around it. A big aviary stood in the middle of the playground; dark shapes hopped and flapped behind the grill. I pulled up by a petrol pump and felt the cool metal on my neck.

"Well?"

"This is Hacking Inlet. I've never been here before. The Gregory's doesn't cover it, and I've only got the name of a lane, not a detailed map."

"So?"

"So we look for the town map or we find someone to ask."

We got out of the car; I'm a city man, but I felt like a country man beside Hayes. I was wearing jeans, a collarless ex-navy shirt and sneakers, he had on his business clothes and business shoes. Dry leaves crackled loudly under his feet as he walked across the clearing.

"Map might be up by the store there," I said.

He judged the distance; a wide verandah ran along the front of the building which was built up on high brick foundations. From where we stood its whole length was visible, framed against the pale moonlit sea. He smiled and lifted his gun.

"Go ahead, Hardy. Go on up and look—I could put one in your ear from here."

I walked over, and climbed the wide wooden steps up to the verandah. It would be a nice place to sit and have a quiet drink in pleasant company, now it felt like a rifle range. My foot hit a beer can lying on the verandah and sent it clattering over the edge. I froze, then looked back at Hayes. He wasn't doing anything stagey; he wasn't standing with his legs spread and his gun arm out supported by the other arm. He was just there and watching.

There was a big, white-edged town plan covered by a cracked sheet of glass mounted on the wall near the door of the shop. I squinted, but I couldn't make out the details. I went back down the steps and over to the car. Hayes lifted his gun and I stopped.

"What's up?"

"Can't see, I need a light."

He nodded and I opened the driver's door: it was lucky that the door-operated interior light hasn't worked for years. I got a torch from the glove box and my gun from the clip. The gun with the two inch barrel went down into the front of my pants, where I prayed it would stay and not show. I flicked the torch on and off experimentally.

"Get on with it!"

I went back to the map and located the lane. Hayes held his hand up ready to shield his eyes against the torch beam if I'd decided to play that trick. His gun hand was rock steady.

"Short drive," I said.

We went down a rocky side road that had been cut into a hill, and off that down a track; the long grass sticking up in the middle between the wheel ruts showed that it didn't get much use. I had the lights on high beam and it was a first-gear crawl along the track. The water was off to the left—a long, flat stretch framed by high, scrubby hills. The tide was low and the water looked like mud; maybe it was. The pylons of a couple of small boat jetties stuck up awkward and useless-looking high above the water line.

"End of the lane here." I was whispering, for no good reason.

"Stay well back then, and turn the car around."

I stopped, backed and filled and got the car turned about in the narrow lane. I'd seen the house in the last flash of the headlights—a narrow-fronted fibro job, just visible through heavy tree-cover. We approached it by going slowly along the side of the track where bushes and saplings offered irregular cover. Ten metres from the house, and to one side, there was a dark patch in the vegetation. I pushed at the low, light branches and they gave way; behind them I could feel, from a step or two taken, firm ground falling away evenly.

"Said to be a driveway down there," I whispered. "Garage holds a couple of cars, store room, God knows what."

Hayes nodded and gestured with the gun for me to come back up on the track. He stepped back to avoid the possible suddenly released branch: he wasn't such a city boy after all. He was a pro. When I was on the track, he grabbed a handful of my hair and jerked my head down. His voice in my ear was hard and harsh: "Listen, Hardy, I've killed eight men. I don't mind killing people. I wouldn't mind killing you. Don't try anything clever. I won't give you a chance. If I get Collinson neat and clean, you've got a chance of getting out of this. Just a chance, get me?"

I nodded, torturing the follicles.

"Right. Now how the fuck do we get in there?"

It was 1:30 A.M. The half-moon went behind a patch of cloud and the scene darkened. The trees that hid the house from the road were thick and high; I could see more of the shack's tin roof from this point than its fibro walls. It was an unpretentious property. The trees on the block grew close around the house, loomed over it. A fire risk. I strained my eyes to see through the trees to what lay beyond the house. Darkness. Then I remembered the water and the jetties. I pointed with the torch butt.

"Looks like this place has got absolute water frontage. Must be a track down to the house from up here, path or something. What d'you reckon on using the torch?"

"Give it to me."

I handed him the torch and he shaded the beam carefully as we picked out way along the track. Hayes stopped and made a pushing gesture. He clicked off the torch.

"Gate. After you."

I went through, inching my way, trying to feel the ground with my toes through the worn-down sneaker soles. I stumbled, flailed my arms, almost fell. Hayes hissed something behind me and I lurched sideways to grab a tree trunk. I poked my foot forward tentatively.

"Path. Goes down. Pretty steep—rocks and roots."

"Go on."

I edged down the path using the trees growing at the sides to steady myself. It was like walking into a downward sloping pitch-black tunnel. Sweat was trickling down my neck, and I felt the gun in my pants move and settle into my crotch. I slid my hand down, pulled up the gun and my shirt front. I put the gun in my pocket, and let the shirt hang in front of it. I slid, bounced off a tree, and stopped.

"Easy," he hissed.

We were at the bottom, standing on a concrete slab that jutted out for about three metres and ran the width of the house. The windows were set high up near the roof, and I thought I could see a gleam of light inside. Windows placed that high seemed strange until I realised that lower windows wouldn't give a view back up to the gate and the track. The house hadn't been designed to be snuck up on.

Hayes stood motionless and seemed to be sniffing the air. All I could hear was a low, sucking sound coming from beyond the front of the house and the soft brushing of bushes, rubbing against the fibro in the light breeze.

The Doberman came quickly and smoothly with a soft footfall and just a low growl. It sprang at Hayes, but he was like a good boxer—he seemed to have all the time in the world. He stepped back and chopped it across the muzzle with his gun hand; the dog yelped and faltered. Hayes pivoted and smashed the gun butt dead-centre on to the dog's skull. The animal quivered and sank and he hit it again, savagely. Its legs gave way and it twitched, heaved, and lay still.

"Had to be one." There was a slight panting in his voice but that was all the effect the bit of action had on him. "Means he's here," he said.

The hair was still sticking up on the back of my neck, but Hayes had moved on to the next step. He examined the back door which was sturdy, set close in its frame, and flush with the wall. It had a newish Chubb Guardian lock.

"Alarm?" I said.

He shook his head. "No point. Don't like this, though. Side."

166

We stepped over the body of the dog and went along the slab to the side of the house. The concrete gave way to wood—a narrow, slatted verandah, with the slats running at right angles to the house. Halfway along, a French window was being softly stroked by a tree branch. A dog's bowl and an old blanket lay on the slats in front of the window.

Hayes bent and slipped off his city shoes; he looked at my feet and nodded. We passed the heavily curtained section of the window, and Hayes picked up the bowl and laid it carefully down on top of the blanket. The menace and purpose of him had me almost mesmerised now. I forgot who he was and what he was doing—his meticulous, precise movements seemed to have a validity of their own that had nothing to do with law and justice. I felt as if I was watching a riveting film with a very good actor in the lead. I fought against the feeling, trying to define my own role. My battered ear was hurting as the cool air nipped at it, and I could feel the gun in my pocket.

Hayes tried the handle on the French window and it turned easily with a slight creak. He shook his head at the carelessness; but Fido was supposed to take care of this entrance, and he'd been taken care of. He opened the glass-paned door and looked in. I was close behind him, but my feeling was that he knew just where I was and what my hands were doing. There was light only at the back of the house; the room we faced was dark and still. Hayes eased the door open until it was at its full swing. He pinned it there with his stockinged foot and motioned me to go in. I looked at him: his face was set, but not tense. I couldn't see any sweat beads at the ex-hairline. His gun moved impatiently and I stepped into Peter Collinson's hideaway.

The room we were in seemed to take up about a third of the floor plan of the house. There was a deep carpet on the floor, and the walls were wood-panelled. A big fireplace divided the wall opposite the French windows, and there were heavy drapes drawn over floor-to-ceiling windows in the wall which formed in front of the house. The glass-paned front door was uncovered.

Hayes and I stood by the open window, breathing softly and adapting to the darkness. The moon moved into the clear and beams of light came through the glass—enough to show the outlines of the furniture, which consisted of a low table in front of the fireplace, an easy chair to the side of it and a hi-fi, radio and TV unit. A set of low shelves held records and cassettes, and there was a large bookcase, well stocked.

Hayes pointed and we moved across the carpet towards the back. The house had a simple lay-out; a galley-style kitchen ran along the whole length of the back section, and we didn't bother to go down the three steps to look in. The single bedroom was off the large front room to the left. The door stood half-open and there was a soft light inside. Hayes moved the slide on the .45 back, cocking it. The mechanism was oiled and smooth and the click was barely audible although I was only a few centimetres away from it.

"Go into the bedroom," he whispered, "and stand in the nearest corner with your face to the wall."

My heart was crashing in my chest and I could feel the blood beating in my temples. The floor felt red hot. I could smell Hayes an arm's length behind me. I went across and sidled through the door, knocking my elbow as I went. Hayes's breath was sibilant by my shoulder. I moved toward the corner as instructed, but it wasn't necessary to go all the way. The night-light was turned very low, barely lifting the gloom, but I could see that there was no one in the bed. I stopped at the foot of the double bed; Hayes stopped too. The bed was rumpled and a pair of track-suit-style pyjamas lay across the single pillow.

"He's not here," I said, stupidly.

"He was."

My legs felt shaky, and I sat down on the end of the bed. Hayes moved forward, picked up an ashtray from the bedside table and looked at the half-dozen butts.

"He was here tonight." He looked at the butts again and at the bed. "Alone."

We prowled through the house and Hayes used the torch, still carefully, to find out what he wanted to know. In the kitchen there was evidence of an evening meal and some after dinner drinking. Collinson had a supply of everything, and all of the best quality. The refrigerator was full of food and drink—meat, cheeses, white wine, beer. The cupboards were stacked with packet and tinned food and everything necessary for successful cooking. There were several dozen bottles of red wine in a rack and a few more cases of the stuff along with spirits and mixers. I felt myself relaxing a little.

"Crime pays," I said. Hayes didn't laugh.

"Where the fuck is he?"

Under the house, reached from a set of steps in the kitchen, was the garage, storeroom, workshop, and boat shed. The food supply was siege-worthy, as Phillips had said. There were two cars in residence—a Mercedes and a battered Holden panel van. Two wide benches held vices, clamps and the equipment for servicing cars and boats. We looked around, both trying to do the same thing—use the information this setup gave us to judge where he might be. My recent minor boat experience gave me the answer.

"Here's the boat stuff," I said. "Where's the boat—speedboat, dinghy, whatever? There's marks here," I squatted on the cement floor, "that shows where he towed a boat up. Probably with the panel van. No boat now."

He nodded. We went back into the house, through it, and out the front door. The water was still at low tide and the mud, or something under it, was making the sucking noise I had heard from the back of the house. There was a small patch of grass in front of the house with some beach scrub fringing it. A jetty about twenty metres long joined the grassy bank, ran over a short belt of sand, and stretched its length out over the moving mud.

Hayes never let his guard down; he dropped behind me and let me lead the way down the jetty. It ended in a wide-planked staging with a hand rail, and steps which would have reached the water at high tide. Now, they finished a metre or so above the heaving, dark mud. There was an almost-empty can of diesel fuel on the top step, and an oily rag hanging over the rail. Hayes, who was wearing his shoes again but had taken off his jacket, bent to examine these items after waving me to a safe distance. The moon was high now in a clear sky and visibility was good. I saw dark, moist circles spreading under Hayes' armpits—his only indisposition; my shirt was a damp rag. He straightened up with clicking bones.

"If he's fishing, Christ knows when he'll be back."

I thought about the house and the garage, checking the items mentally.

170

"No fishing gear anywhere," I said. "No fish in the freezer. He's not a fisherman. He'll be back for breakfast. He likes to eat. Probably feeds the birds, too."

Hayes turned to look back at the house. It was shadowed by the trees growing close to it and the foliage spread out unbroken to either side. There were houses further up the hill, but none so close to the water.

The shoreline was rocky for most of the cove and there were no other houses with such direct access to the water until further around the points off to the east and west. When Collinson came back he'd be pulling up to a private jetty in a semi-private setting. His tying-up point would be well below the main section of the jetty, virtually invisible to all except someone who cared to station himself in the scrub to the right. Such a person would be twenty metres from the boat landing, in concealment and unobstructed. If it happened like that, Collinson was a dead man. I took all this in quickly and Hayes obviously did the same. His usually grim expression—something like a cross between a headmaster's and a bookie's—relaxed a fraction. You couldn't call it a smile.

"Say he gets back at dawn," he said. "When's that down here, with your godless daylight saving?"

"About five."

"Say, three hours to wait, bit less. I can wait that long for half a million bucks. Couldn't you, Hardy?"

"I'm never likely to get the chance."

"That's right. You're not. Did you enjoy hitting Liam with the bottle?"

"Not really. A bit, I suppose."

"You should've enjoyed it a lot! And not given a bugger at the same time. That's what being hard is all about."

"Psychology, now."

"We had lectures. Most of the dead-heads didn't get anything out of them. I did."

171

I didn't have anything to say to that. We walked back along the jetty across the grass to the house.

Inside, Hayes undid his top collar-button and loosened his tie. He motioned at me to sit on the floor and he lowered himself into the easy chair.

"I'm tired," he said. "I'm bloody tired, but I can't afford to drop off. I've learned a few tricks in my time—know the most important?"

I shook my head.

"Don't drink at the wrong time. I'd love a drink; and did you see all that good stuff he's got out there?"

"Yeah, I saw it."

"I'll have one after he's dead. At the right time."

"Like Jackie Gleason?" I said.

"What?"

"Jackie Gleason, in a movie called *The Hustler*. He plays this pool champ called Minnesota Fats, has a big game with Paul Newman. Newman gets pissed when he's ahead; Gleason doesn't drink, washes up in the break and creams him. Jackie Gleason's fatter than you, but you're getting there—six months of the good life should do it."

"We'll see. I hope you don't think of yourself as Paul-fucking-Newman?"

"No."

"That's good. Know another little trick? Keep talking when you're tired. Keep your company talking. You're doing fine, Hardy. Keep talking. You're a great talker, aren't you?"

"I'm a fair talker. Why did you bring Catchpole and his crowd into this?"

"Useful. Dottie was supposed to get a girl for Ray. Ended up doing the job herself. She tried to get him to talk about Collinson, his real father."

"How did that go?"

172

"Not good. Very cagey. He said he'd come across with things, like that photo. We told him we'd help him to locate his old man. 'Course, it was the other way around. Liam's got contacts in the New South Wales force, more than people realise. He did a bit of this and a bit of that. My turn—why d'you do this shit-kicking kind of work?"

"It's not bad. Bit dull at times."

"Not dull now, eh?"

"No."

"You reckon you're going to survive this?"

I didn't like the way the talk was going; he was playing with me and I felt clumsy-witted. The chance of getting him off-balance seemed remote.

"Well, do you?"

"I don't know," I said. "You tell me."

He yawned. "Depends how it goes."

"How else can it go? You said yourself you could shoot a man's ear off at that range and in those conditions. If he comes, he's dead, isn't he?"

He almost grinned. "He might have a gun—like you."

"What?"

He made the pseudo-laughing noise again. This time it sounded like the gurgling mud outside. "I saw you get it from the car. Saw you switch it to your pocket. But you didn't have the guts to use it, did you?"

"Biding my time."

"Well you waited too long, sonny Jim. Just ease it out slowly, put it on the floor, and give it a kick over here."

I did what he said, and I had the odd sensation that my body temperature had dropped when I surrendered the gun. I shivered, although it wasn't cold; my throat was dry and it closed on me when I tried to speak. The fear was back.

"What was that again?" His voice was full of mock concern and politeness.

"Why'd you wait so long to get the gun, Hayes?"

"Just having fun."

"That's not professional."

"Well, in fact I figured you'd play along more if you thought you had an edge. It worked."

We sat in silence for a while, then he shifted in his chair.

"Know the best way to stay awake when you're tired, Hardy?"

"No."

"Concentrate on your bladder. Tell yourself you need a piss. Pretty soon you will. That gives you something to think about. You don't have the piss and you stay awake."

"I could do with a piss right now."

"Me too. But you can have one. Get up!"

I climbed off the floor and we went back to the toilet which was off the kitchen. I pissed, zipped up, and when I turned around he had a couple of lengths of light rope in his hand.

"Right, Hardy. Into the bedroom. We're going to wrap you up for a while."

He instructed me to get on the bed; he tossed me one of the pieces of rope and supervised me while I tied up my legs. Then he tied my hands behind me, and tightened up the knots all round, like a man tightening the wheel nuts on a car.

"Why?" I said.

"Who knows? Hostage maybe. I keep my options open. Goodbye, Hardy."

He clicked off the night-light, and closed the door.

20

Lying there on the bed in the darkness, head down and arse up, the Chesterton quotation, or something of it, came into my head—to do with fucking: "The position is ridiculous, the expense damnable." I used to think it was funny, but it didn't seem so funny anymore.

By cranking my neck around and lifting my head, I could just get a look out a window where a holland blind ended a fraction above the sill. It was still very dark out and I wasn't anxious for it to get light. After a while the birds started up in the trees—incongruously happy chirpings. I cranked and lifted again, but it still wasn't dawn or even pre-dawn. My arms quickly got cramped and sore, and the split skin on my ear was throbbing. I wondered whether it really had been a lack of guts that had kept me from trying to use the gun on Hayes, or was it an instinct for survival. Or were they both the same thing?

The door opened; I felt the wind of it rather than heard any noise. I went tense and my jaw clamped tight. So did my eyes, and the back of my neck tingled. I couldn't see why he'd get impatient and do it now, but who could tell how a Queensland cop turned hit-man, who'd killed eight people, was likely to think? I expected to hear a noise; I hoped that'd be all.

"Hardy! Hardy!" The voice was Frank Parker's, but it sounded sweeter than Cleo Laine.

I grunted something unintelligible even to me.

"Lie still," he whispered. "And for Christ's sake, don't fall off the bed when you're loose."

He undid the knots and I rolled over and sat up. Parker was wearing one of my denim shirts and dark pants. He'd daubed something on his face to cut down on skin shine at night. *Christ, I can see him*, I thought. It must be getting light. I strained my ears but couldn't pick up any boat noise.

"How?" I said.

"I watched your place most of the day. Thought Catchpole'd show up. I got the word to him that you lifted Tiny."

"Thanks! You're a ruthless bastard, Frank."

"Worked, didn't it? I wasn't expecting Hayes to come into the bag. Is this place what I think it is?"

"It's Collinson's bolthole."

"Uh huh. Where's 'Bully'?"

"Christ, you don't know?"

"No. I lay low for a while trying to work out what was going on—saw out the front and decided to nip in to get you out. Where is he?"

"He's out in the scrub, waiting for Collinson who should be coming over the horizon in a boat pretty soon." I scratched at my own cheek. "What's this, bit of drama?"

"Yeah. Do you want your gun?"

"Shit, yes!"

He gave it to me. "How'd he get it off you?"

The relief I was feeling almost made me giggle. "He asked me nicely. I'm telling you, Frank, this guy is good. He's got a perfect setup out there for blowing Collinson away." I got off the bed and swore as my calf muscle cramped.

"You okay? We'd better get out there."

"Right." I rubbed the leg and hobbled. "Have you seen the kid?"

Parker shook his head. He had his gun ready, and mine in my hand felt huge. *Bloody guns*, I thought, but the time had come now. We went into the front room: the pre-dawn light was lifting in the sky, visible through the uncurtained front door. The water level was up; the jetty looked solidly based now, ready to serve its purpose.

"Can't go through here," I said. "He could be keeping an eye out."

Parker nodded, and moved toward the side door we'd all used. We edged along the verandah to the front of the house, but it was hard to get far enough forward to look along the scrub without being seen.

We crouched behind a bush, maybe ten feet from where Hayes would be, maybe closer. The water lapped at the narrow strip of greyish sand, slapped at the jetty pylons. Parker shook his head.

"We step out there, and we're dead. He'd see us long before we'd spot him. We'll have to wait for Collinson to come before we can move. Hope for some confusion, or start some."

"He's not the easily confused type. Did you see the dog?"

"Yeah."

I mimed the three chopping blows Hayes had used on the Doberman, and Parker sucked his teeth.

There was nothing in the clear, pale sky to impede the flood of light as the sun came up. The dull, leaden look of the water receded toward the shadows on the far side of the cove, and a deep green spread across the surface.

The sound started as a dull hum, scarcely audible above the noise of the water and the busy birds. The boat appeared from around a headland, perhaps a kilometre away and it came in rapidly, skipping slightly in the light waves, headed directly toward the jetty. Parker tensed beside me and we both edged forward, almost breaking cover, straining to see the man sitting in the stern of the boat.

He cut the motor a few metres from the jetty and let her drift in. He looked huge sitting there, and I realised he was

177

wearing a life vest and a quilted jacket over that. As a target for Hayes, it couldn't have been better. The boatman had just begun to gather himself to stand and throw a rope to the jetty when a shout came from the scrub away to the right.

"Hey! In the boat!"

Parker judged it exactly right: the voice was light, he must have realised it wasn't Hayes, and he moved out fast with his gun up. I was a beat behind him and my eyes flicked along the scrub line, trying to see Hayes. Further along, Ray Guthrie had taken several steps out on to the sand. He lifted his hand to wave and he yelled again. The man in the boat ducked down and scrabbled for something at his feet. Then I saw Hayes; he was on his feet with his pistol up and levelled.

Parker shot him: Hayes spun around at the impact of the first shot, but Parker adjusted instantly, and got him twice more as he was going back and down. Ray Guthrie stood stock still on the beach as the sound of the shots crashed across the water.

It was a trick of the light or a moment in history or whatever you want to call it, but with his hand up in alarm near his face and with his head half-ducked away from the shots, Ray looked uncannily like the Digger in the faded photograph of thirty years before.

I sprinted down the jetty to the landing; Collinson had pulled up a carbine from the bottom of the boat, but the drama on the beach had distracted him. I pointed the .38 down at his padded chest.

"That's your son Ray on the beach," I said. "He just saved your life. Put the gun down, it's over."

He was bigger than he looked in the photograph with a craggy, sun-tanned face and strong white teeth Hilde would have admired. He was looking at Ray and scarcely seemed to notice me. But he put the carbine down.

"Out!"

His boat was still drifting. He looped a rope over a short

post on the staging and pulled her in. He was wearing khaki pants and thong sandals which slapped the steps as he came up. We went along the jetty to the grass. Ray Guthrie had scrambled up there from the sand. His father walked toward him. They looked at each other and I stood back to let them have their meeting.

"Ray," Collinson said.

Ray nodded.

Collinson clapped him on the upper arm. "You look good. We'll talk."

Ray nodded again. Collinson dropped down on to the sand and walked over to where Parker was standing, looking down at "Bully" Hayes. I followed Collinson.

Hayes was on his back. Parker's head shot had wrecked one side of his face. He'd done up his collar again, and pulled up the tie—the formality looked odd on a corpse. The expensive shirt had a big, ochre-coloured stain from armpit to waist on one side, and the convulsive twist he'd given when he went down had pulled half of the tail out of his pants. His belly swelled under a cotton singlet. There was nothing menacing about him now, nothing special. He looked ordinary.

Ray Guthrie had followed us over and I turned around to look at him. He'd shaved off the drooping moustache, and that had restored his youth to him; he was dirty, his face was scratched. He looked at me puzzled, trying to place me.

"Saw you in Brisbane," I said. "I didn't do anything to your brother."

He drew in a deep breath; some of the weight had gone off him quickly, and his cheeks were hollowed by strain and fatigue. "All right," he said.

Collinson heard this and jerked his head at me. "The other boy, Chris, he's not part of this bloody shambles, is he?"

"He is," I said.

"What's happened to him?"

"He's all right. His mother's with him now, so's his stepfather. You'll hear all about it." I looked down at Hayes again. "It was worth half a million dollars to him to kill you."

Collinson sniffed loudly and rubbed his hand across his grey-stubbled face. "Getting a cold. That much, eh? Who was he?"

"Name's Hayes," Parker said. "Henry Hayes, from Queensland."

Collinson sniffed again. "And who're you?"

"I'm Detective Sergeant Frank Parker, Homicide Division, and I'm arresting you for the murder of Charles Barratt."

Collinson didn't waste breath or movement; he twisted suddenly, like a cat. He jerked my gun away and tipped me off balance. He levelled the gun at Parker.

"Come on, Ray," he barked. "Let's go!"

Ray stared at his father who'd dropped into a semi-crouch; with his face grey and grimacing he looked like a cornered animal. Ray slowly shook his head.

Collinson straightened up and backed off toward the house. I took one long step toward him.

"Stop!" He moved the gun like an expert.

I ducked and dashed forward. The flash and crack were very close but I rammed into him with my shoulder dropped and elbow digging in. He fell hard; Parker kicked the gun away and we held him down while he struggled, briefly.

"Okay," he said. "Okay. Get off me."

We all stood up and Parker covered him carefully. I picked up my gun and flicked sand off it.

"Bloody fool," Parker said.

I grinned at him. "No risk. This thing shoots high and a mile right. If you don't know that you can't hit a house with it."

21

I stood guard over Collinson and Ray Guthrie, although they didn't need much guarding. They talked quietly the whole time. I caught snatches of the conversation—the topics included boats, Chris and Pat Guthrie, and the Korean and Vietnam Wars. I got Ray aside briefly and he told me that he'd followed the same route to Hacking Inlet as me—via Ian Style and Joshua Phillips. It'd been a good day for Phillips, because Ray had given him forty dollars. A stolen car had brought him from Sydney and he'd spent most of the night in the scrub wondering at the goings on.

"Ray, Catchpole, and Dottie were working on you to get at Collinson." We were in the front room and Collinson was in the easy chair. I jerked by head at him. "You see that, do you?"

"Yes. I just couldn't get along with Dad . . . Guthrie. I tried, but it just got harder. I felt as if I'd been born aged ten or something. Couldn't stand it. But he hired you to look out for me, did he?"

"Paul Guthrie did, yes."

He shook his head wearily and I left him to chew on it.

Frank spent more than an hour on the telephone. Between making calls and answering them, he explained the problem. "For everyone who wants him alive and talking, there's one who wants him dead and quiet."

"His chances don't sound good."

"They're only fair. He'd know that."

"Are we going to have to go back to town incognito—disguises, all that shit?"

He laughed. "No. Not if the right word comes through." He rattled the telephone. It rang again soon after, and he listened and grunted by turns. It was boring to listen to and I wandered off after a while. After the tension and drama I felt flat and let-down. It was only to do with money after all—big money, but just money.

The day got started and promised to be a spectacular one. The water outside the house rippled and shone, and Collinson's boat tossed gently at the rope's end. If you could forget that there was a man with flies on his face twenty metres away, it looked like a cheerful scene.

"Hey, Frank, did you cover Hayes?"

He waved me to silence. He was on the phone again, intensely responding and high strung. He nodded, said "Yes" several times, and put the phone down. He sagged back against the wall and scraped at the commando marks on his face. "It looks okay," he muttered. "Cross your fingers, but it looks okay."

I never did learn the full details—just which Deputy Commissioner said what to who; which Attorney General's department man spoke to which judge. But men and vehicles started arriving; Collinson was taken away and Parker went into several huddles with men in suits. There was a little shouting. I was starting to recover my pragmatism and I insisted on informal custody of Ray Guthrie, and no one objected. Paul Guthrie had spoken of a bonus, and the fine, bright day brought fine, bright thoughts of Helen.

I phoned her and her deep, controlled voice seemed to be coming from another world after the male near-hysteria I'd been witness to.

"How're you?" she said—ordinary words, but they sounded as though she really meant it.

"I'm fine, and it's over. Hope you didn't mind me putting Jess on you."

"I'm glad you did. She's a good kid. Is her bloke all right?"

"He's okay, been through a bit. He'd like to talk to her."

"Put him on."

I kicked my heels impatiently while Ray got all post-adolescent on the phone for ten minutes. He was smiling when he handed the receiver over to me.

"Hurry back," Helen said.

After that, Ray flaked on Collinson's bed for a while. I got a bottle of white wine out of the fridge, and went out with Frank on the jetty for a late morning bracer. He rinsed his mouth with the wine and spat it into the water. It was no way to treat good riesling, but he'd had a hard night. He was favouring his left side, but it hadn't bothered him during the action.

"Wonder what happened to Liam and Dottie?" I said.

"Still going south if they've got any sense."

"I was supposed to drop the tail at the park entrance."

"Child's play, spotted it easy."

"What about at the turn-off the park road?"

"Old cop trick. Keep going and come back."

"Are you back where you want to be?"

"Looks that way. How's your employer going to take all this?"

I drank some wine and considered the question.

"He's got a few knocks coming, but you saw him; he can take it. He won't like Collinson surfacing too much."

Parker sipped, and swallowed this time. "I held out on you, Cliff. I've got a crumb you can throw Guthrie."

I looked at him and didn't speak.

He drank another mouthful. "Better stuff than at your place. Well, according to the file, Collinson went through a form of marriage with Patricia Ramsay. He was married before, and that second marriage was bigamous. That means Guthrie's marriage is valid."

"So it does. Well, that could be worth something."

When the last official had gone, and the house had been sealed and all the evidence collected, I shook hands with Parker and watched him climb into an official car. There was activity on the hill above the house; I saw the flash of field glasses and a few brave souls had even come down the lane to ask what was going on. Nobody told them anything. A couple of boats cruised around in the cove and one pulled up at Collinson's landing. I walked halfway down the jetty, made shoo-ing motions and the boat puttered off. Collinson's flash motor boat was still tied up; when the tide went out it'd sit stranded on the mud like a car with two flats.

Ray was waiting for me and we got into my car and drove back to Elizabeth Bay. We didn't talk; I was tired from the sleepless night and a bit light-headed from the wine. I felt the city drawing me, but the miles went by slowly as if each was a bit longer than the last.

Jess Polansky was still at Helen's place. She and Ray thanked Helen and thanked me, and took themselves off.

Helen stood at her window and watched them walk down the street. I came over and kissed her. She was wearing a black silk shirt and white pants. She winced when I put my hand on her back to pull her closer.

"What's wrong?"

"Sunburn, from the skinny dipping."

"Sorry."

She touched the cut on my ear which had a sticking plaster over it and it was my turn to wince.

"Sorry," she said.

We did some more kissing, and moved away from the window and the bright street and sea to the cool dimness of her bedroom.

After, she sat up in bed and pulled the sheet up over her breasts. I looked up at her shapely back which was just slightly red where the newly exposed skin had been burnt.

"What?" I said.

"You know I said my year off was coming up for its half-yearly review?"

"Yes."

"I've decided. I'm taking the second half."